"Kisses can't happen again, Jake.

Not if we want to work together. I'm not your type and you're not my type. I don't want a broken heart."

"We've got a business agreement, and I don't think sex and business mix well. Sticking to business is not impossible to do," he said and smiled. "I've never crossed that line before."

Emily smiled in return and hoped she could live up to her speech.

She couldn't forget his kiss—ever. She wanted to walk right back into his arms now, but she wasn't going to. Because that would lead to heartbreak. It would be too easy to fall in love with him, the deep and forever kind of love.

* * *

The Forbidden Texan is part of the Texas Promises series from *USA TODAY* bestselling author Sara Orwig.

Dear Reader,

I feel the men and women in the United States military are special because they risk their lives protecting our country and our beliefs. This is the third book about patriotic Texas ranchers who joined the military. The three are US Army rangers, and when their captain and buddy is critically wounded, each ranger promises to fulfill his dying friend's request. Being honorable men, they keep their promises, even when each one finds it requires doing something he doesn't want to do.

When billionaire Texas rancher Jake Ralston goes home, he must keep his promise to hire an antiques dealer to help him dispose of belongings in a ranch house he inherited from his deceased captain. For over a century, Emily Kincaid's and Jake Ralston's families have had a bitter feud, and Jake feels he has promised the impossible by working daily on an isolated ranch with Emily. To their dismay, they have an unwanted sizzling attraction that complicates their lives.

I hope you enjoy this story of the third Texas promise. Please visit my author page on Facebook: Sara Orwig, Romance Writer. I would love to hear from you.

Sara Orwig

SARA ORWIG

THE FORBIDDEN TEXAN

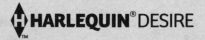

Recycling programs
for this product may
not exist in your area.

ISBN-13: 978-1-335-60339-5

The Forbidden Texan

Copyright © 2018 by Sara Orwig

Printed in U.S.A.

www.Harlequin.com

Married to the guy she met in college, *USA TODAY* bestselling author **Sara Orwig** has three children and six grandchildren. Sara has published 109 novels. One of the first six inductees into the Oklahoma Professional Writers Hall of Fame, Sara has twice won Oklahoma Novel of the Year. Sara loves family, friends, dogs, books, beaches and Dallas, Texas.

Books by Sara Orwig

Harlequin Desire

Callahan's Clan

Expecting the Rancher's Child
The Rancher's Baby Bargain
The Rancher's Cinderella Bride
The Texan's Baby Proposal

Texas Promises

Expecting a Lone Star Heir
The Forbidden Texan
The Rancher's Heir

Visit her Author Profile page at Harlequin.com, or saraorwig.com, for more titles.

To senior editor Stacy Boyd
with thanks for being my editor.

To Maureen Walters for all you do.

To my family with love.

One

In September, as Jake Ralston flew to Texas, he was lost in thoughts about the deathbed promise he'd made to his late friend and army ranger captain, Thane Warner. He hadn't been expecting to return home and face a bitter enemy, but now he was flying back to Dallas to do just that.

Flying into DFW, Jake saw the orange glow in the night sky and then the twinkling lights of the city. He had finally finished his three years with the army and he was headed home.

He'd celebrated with military friends right after he was released. Now, on Saturday, the first day of September, he would be staying at his Dallas condo so he could see his family tonight.

Tomorrow night he'd celebrate at a welcome home party with his local friends. He was ready for a party. Parties, pretty women and peace. He was looking forward to all three. As a member of the army rangers, he'd done his part to help keep peace and now he was going back to his civilian life.

He planned to live on his Hill Country ranch, but his family's business interests were in Dallas. He would divide his time between the two places.

The only part of the war that was left in his life was his promises to his buddy—and the first promise was a whopper. He was to hire a woman whose family hadn't spoken to his family in over a century and a half.

Before he could make good on that promise to Thane and hire Emily Kincaid, he first had to get her to talk to him. No easy feat. He hadn't spoken to a Kincaid in ten years—since he beat Emily's oldest brother, Doug, in saddle bronc riding at an Amarillo rodeo when he was twenty-two. Before that, it was another brother, Lucas, with whom he'd fought way back in high school. If he had his druthers, he wouldn't have been dealing with any Kincaid, but he'd promised Thane and he was an honorable man. He'd just have to get this job out of the way as fast as possible.

He barely knew Emily Kincaid. He knew she was a professional appraiser and she was younger than he was—but that was it. A vague mental picture came to mind when she was a skinny girl with pigtails.

One thing he did know well. Getting a Kincaid to work for a Ralston was going to be next to impossible. Except for two things. Emily and Thane had been friends. And Thane had left a cashier's check for a small fortune to bribe Emily. Would the money sway her? Or, perhaps, would her friendship with Thane compel her to honor his memory? Jake would find out soon enough.

Thane Warner had been a top-notch soldier, had had an amazing influence on his ranger team and everyone he met throughout his life. He'd made life-long friends easily—and Jake counted himself among the many.

So nearly two years ago, when Thane lay dying in Afghanistan and called for his ranger buddies who were ambushed with him—one by one to instruct them of his wishes—they all promised to honor him. Mike Moretti, Noah Grant and Jake. The first two had carried through his plans to the letter. Now it was Jake's turn.

He still felt the sting of Thane's loss. It wasn't survivor guilt; it was genuine grief. Of a life cut short. Of a good friend lost. Jake couldn't imagine the pain his family must be feeling.

Now that he was home, he wanted to go see the Warners, to offer his condolences and reminisce with those who knew him best. Growing up, he'd spent hours at Thane's house, which had been a far more harmonious place than his own home. Thane's dad had been a better dad to him than any of Jake's stepfathers or his biological father, and Thane's mother was sweet. Jake had half siblings but he didn't feel as close to any of them as he always had with Thane. He was going to miss his friend.

Thane, too, had had a high opinion of Jake. But in this instance, Jake thought, Thane was asking him to do the impossible: end the Ralston-Kincaid feud. That feud started about 1864, give or take a couple of years, and according to the stories, those early years were wild, with murders and thefts, one hanging and duels, one of which involved his great-great-great-grandfather. How was Jake going to be able to end years of hatred between two families? *Make friends with them*, Thane had whispered when Jake had asked that question. That wasn't going to happen. Jake would be lucky if he could get Emily Kincaid to be civil to him, let alone agree to work for him.

After all, unlike Jake, Emily hadn't promised Thane anything.

Emily Kincaid glanced at the clock. Five more minutes till her appointment with Jake Ralston. Though she didn't want any dealings with a Ralston, this one she had to see. Because he was bringing a letter to her from Thane. She had grown up knowing Thane Warner. He had been eight years older and friends with her older brothers, but he was always nice to her. It had saddened her to hear of his death in Afghanistan nearly two years ago. His widow, Vivian, had remarried a United States Army Ranger who had served with Thane. Because of her antiques-and-appraisal business, Emily had worked with Vivian, an artist, and Emily liked her.

Emily glanced at the clock again, curious and, admittedly, nervous about her upcoming meeting. While she wasn't as into the feud as some members of her family, she rarely spoke to any Ralston. Tempers ran higher with the Kincaid and Ralston ranchers. It was with the ranchers where the past was violent and ugly.

Still, she thought it best to talk to Jake in the privacy of her office, which was in the back corner of her store, so most Kincaids would never even know she'd associated with a Ralston.

The buzz of her intercom interrupted her thoughts and her assistant announced her visitor.

"Send him in, please," Emily said, standing and walking around her desk. She knew who he was and not much more than that.

Leslie opened the door. "Emily, here is Jake Ralston," the slender brunette said and stepped aside.

Emily was surprised when the tall, handsome

man in a navy Western-style suit, a black broad-brimmed hat and black boots entered the office carrying a briefcase. In person, Jake Ralston was far more good-looking than his pictures in the newspapers and magazines indicated, and he had an air about him that instantly commanded attention.

His startling dark brown eyes caught and held Emily's gaze, and for a moment she wasn't aware of anything else except the tall man facing her. Somehow she managed to get control of herself and, as usual when she met a likely customer, she held out her hand.

"I'm Emily Kincaid. Way back as kids we probably met," she said. If they had met as adults, she would have remembered him. There was no way she could have forgotten meeting him. His warm hand closed firmly around hers and tingles raced up her arm from his touch.

Startled by her reaction, she looked up at him in time to see a flicker of surprise in those dark eyes. Had he felt something, too? His eyes narrowed a fraction when he looked more intently at her. She felt as if all breath had left her lungs and there was no air in the room, only a sizzling current between her and Jake Ralston. After a moment, she realized they were standing in silence, staring at each other and still holding hands.

She yanked her hand away and turned with an

effort. "Please, have a seat," she said, or hoped she said. Her pulse raced and there was a roaring in her ears. What had caused the intense response to him? She didn't react to men in this manner and she didn't know him at all. Besides, he was a Ralston. A Ralston should have been the last person on earth who could elicit a steamy response by a mere handshake.

Trying to regain her composure, she motioned with her hand for him to sit in one of the two leather chairs in front of her desk. She took the one opposite him. Never before had the chairs seemed particularly close, but now she felt she had made a tactical mistake and she should have put her desk between them. She wouldn't even have kept this appointment if she had known she would have this kind of reaction to him. He was handsome, but this startling physical response went way beyond attraction. There was a chemistry that made her feel as if sparks were flying around them.

He tossed his black hat on another chair, revealing thick, slightly wavy black hair, and crossed his long legs. She recognized his black boots as elegant hand-tooled, fine leather dress boots, not work boots. In fact, she noticed everything about him.

She didn't want this kind of reaction to a Ralston. She felt an urgent need to find out what he wanted and get him out of her office.

"Thanks for accepting this appointment. Unless things changed drastically while I was away in the army, you and I are breaking more than a century of silence between our two families. Except for unfriendly communications," he said, looking slightly amused. His dark eyes seemed to hold a degree of curiosity, as if he were eager to notice her as well, although she couldn't imagine that she would stir such a reaction in him as he had in her.

She decided to cut to the chase. "I can't guess any reason why Thane Warner would write to me."

"I won't keep you in suspense. He wanted me to do some things for him that he wasn't going to get to come home and do himself. Important things to him. Thane wanted to get rid of his grandfather's ranch, which he had inherited. Thane said there are valuable things in the house, and he told me that you, Emily, would know the appraised value and where to get rid of what I don't want. He told me about your store, Antiques, Art and Appraisals. I noticed some interesting items as I walked through."

"I've grown up around antiques and being in this business, I have a chance to buy and sell them."

"Thane was badly wounded and we were under fire," Jake said, his voice changing, sounding harsher. "You don't say no to a dying buddy's request. And he was a friend of mine all my life. Without hesitation, I promised I'd do whatever he asked. He actually made three requests and he did ask the impossible. I'll just do the best I can."

She listened to Jake talk and knew he was hurting over the loss of his friend. And she could understand why he couldn't have said no to whatever Thane had requested. She took another deep breath because she had a feeling something was coming that she would want to say no to and Jake Ralston had promised Thane he would get her to agree to do it. She hadn't promised Thane anything, but Jake had already set her up for a guilty conscience if she declined. She wished she could end this appointment without hearing what Jake wanted.

"Thane wanted me to hire you, so I'm offering you a job."

How could she possibly agree to that? She was a Kincaid. She couldn't work for a Ralston. That would stir all kinds of trouble with her family, especially her brothers. She didn't mind talking to Jake in her shop, but working closely with him, going through belongings out on a ranch, was a far more personal involvement with a Ralston.

"Jake, let me stop you right there. I have to say no. Our families are too divided. Feelings are bitter and run high. I can give you names of some really good appraisers who are trustworthy people with lots of experience in this business."

He put both feet on the floor, his elbows on his knees, and leaned forward while she talked until he was almost touching her. She looked into his intent dark eyes that made her heart beat faster.

"Emily," he said in a deep voice that had her attention riveted, "Thane made a supreme effort to stay alive long enough to tell me what he wanted me to do. The medics were astounded he lasted as long as he did. This project was vital to him and he died with my word that I would hire you. I'll do whatever it takes to make that happen. If the only thing standing in the way is an old family feud that you and I are not very involved in, we can manage. I'm not asking you to become my friend, just my employee."

She closed her eyes as he talked and wanted to shut him out of her life, to cover her ears and not hear what he was saying. She didn't want to work for a Ralston out on a ranch. Jake was the best-looking man in the next twelve counties, and from what she had read and heard, he was a man who went through women in amazing numbers. A guy who liked pretty women, loved parties and had no intention of settling into family life. Definitely not her type. Granted, the women she had known who had gone out with him stayed friends, liked him and would be willing to go out with him again if they had the chance. But Emily didn't want to be a trophy or a statistic. She didn't want an affair and she definitely didn't want a broken heart. If she got deeply involved with a man, she was old-fashioned enough that she wanted a wedding ring on her finger.

"Emily, let's go through this before you flatly refuse," he said in a throaty, coaxing voice that sent warmth through her, causing her refusal to fizzle.

"As I said, in the last moments of Thane's life, he asked me to promise him three things—first, to clear out the possessions in his grandfather's ranch house. For promising to do what Thane asked, he deeded that ranch to me as a gift. It is my house and my ranch now. The second promise was to hire you to appraise the contents of the house and help dispose of or keep what we find—and to live at the ranch with me for the duration of this job. The third promise, I'm afraid, is hopeless. It is to try to end the Ralston-Kincaid feud. You and I are talking to each other, making a deal with each other, so that's a start. He did say *try* on that one.

"Let me briefly tell you about my military buddies. Thane was our captain and he was also our friend, fellow Texas rancher and businessman. Although you're younger, you've grown up knowing the Warners and I imagine you know Noah Grant, or at least his sister, Stefanie."

Emily nodded. "I've gone to school with Stefanie and I know the Grants."

"Noah was asked to deliver a letter to the woman who turned out to be the mother of his son. Another Texan fit into our little group, Mike Moretti.

Thane had asked Mike to work at the Tumbling T when Mike returned home. Not only had he done that, he ended up marrying Thane's widow and taking over the ranch. The ranch that sat right in a stateside battlefield—directly between a family of Ralstons and a family of Kincaids."

"I agree that ending the feud is absolutely impossible," Emily replied. "Some of my family members have strong feelings. They wouldn't even want to learn that I'm working for you. Thane was a very nice person, but this job is just not—"

Jake held up his hand, stopping her.

"Hear me out and let me give you the letter and an envelope Thane had for you. As I said, you can't imagine the effort he made to tell me and two of his close friends what he wanted and to get each of us to promise to do certain things."

"With great reluctance, I'll listen," she said, feeling caught between Thane's last wishes and the plea from Jake on Thane's behalf.

"Good," Jake said, giving her another look that took her breath away. She hated his request and watched as he picked up his briefcase, opened it and removed a sealed envelope.

With misgivings, she reached out to take it and as her fingers brushed his hand, she had that instant awareness of contact. She looked up to meet his curious gaze and she felt an uncustomary flash of desire, as unwanted as the envelope in her hand. Why had she agreed to meet with Jake Ralston?

She opened the letter and looked up. "I might as well read this to you, too, because it has to be about my working for you."

"Go ahead," Jake said.

"Dear Emily,
I have asked my friend Jake Ralston to hire you to do the appraisal of my grandfather's belongings and to live with and help Jake dispose and take care of those things. I know it is life changing to ask a Ralston and a Kincaid to work together, but it is temporary, a job with two honorable, trustworthy people working together to do what I am not going to be able to do myself. Please be kind and honor this request of mine. It's time the Kincaids and the Ralstons bury the old battles. Your lives are before both of you and this is a small request, and it will not take a lot of your time. I hope if you agree, that this task will bless both of you and bring something good into your lives. Life is precious, so please don't waste it on an old feud that really doesn't matter. I'd give anything to have that chance. Thank you so very much for doing this. I thank you both. May your lives be filled with joy.
Thane."

When she looked up to meet Jake's gaze, he looked away, but she had seen how the letter had refreshed the pain of losing his friend. Silence stretched between them for a few moments until she spoke. "I suppose you better tell me what it is you want me to do."

"I have a letter, too, with very specific instructions, which we can get into later. In the meantime," he said, removing another envelope from his briefcase, "Thane instructed me to open this envelope, which is from him to you. It's his gift to you for taking the job and he wanted me to know about it. In addition to what's in this envelope, I'll pay you the regular fee for your work. Let me know your fee and we'll go from there." He held out the envelope to her. "Just so that you know, he wrote that Vivian knows and approves of what's in here."

When she took the envelope from him, his fingers brushed hers again and that sharp awareness made her glance up into an intense brown-eyed stare that caused her pulse to jump. What chemistry did they have between them? Unwanted chemistry. She didn't want to be attracted to a Ralston or have her heart flutter by a simple brush of fingers. And he felt it, too. It showed in a revealing flicker in his eyes. Sparks flying between them would make working for him challenging. And definitely something she shouldn't do.

There were a dozen reasons to turn down this

job. She had great respect for Thane Warner, but this wasn't a job she could accept.

She looked down at a brown cnvelope that was wrinkled, smudged, had small tearstains, but was still intact. She pulled open the flap that wasn't sealed and withdrew a cashier's check. "You said you know what's in here."

"Yes, I do. I still have Thane's note that said to open it and look." He paused as she looked down at the check in her hand.

Stunned, she stared at the check, unable to process the zeroes she was seeing. "Good heavens. Is this real?"

"Absolutely. Thane has paid you a million dollars to do this job."

"I can't accept that much money for a job like this."

Jake shrugged. "Thane's not alive. He can't use it. Vivian has inherited his estate worth multimillions. Besides, she's a billionaire heiress with a successful art career and Thane's thriving ranch that her new husband, Mike Moretti, will make even better. She won't need the money. It's yours if you'll take this job."

Stunned, Emily looked at the check, thinking about what he had just said, about where else the money might be used to benefit others. "I'm shocked. I can't even grasp this. Why would he do this?"

"He wanted you to take this job. My guess is that he thought you would turn me down without a good reason to do the appraisal. If we work together, our families will know it. If you take this job, this is the beginning of the end of a feud that is over a century and a half old."

In that moment, Emily realized she could not possibly turn down this job. Her gaze met Jake's. She was going to live under the same roof with the handsome rancher facing her. A charmer, a man who loved beautiful women, parties and no ties. Could she live in the same house with him, work with him every day for the coming month or however long it took, and keep from falling in love with him? Could she work with him and avoid a broken heart? Could she do this and avoid seduction?

Two

Jake had watched her read the check and when all color drained from her face, he had known Thane would get part of what he wanted. She would take the job. Jake was poised to catch her because for a moment she looked on the verge of fainting, which surprised him since she was well-fixed in her own right. Not only did she have her own successful appraisal company, but her family had old money. They had Kincaid Energy, an oil company, and her dad was still CEO, her brother Doug was COO and her brother Will was an executive, too. Lucas had a ranch, but was on the board and was in Dallas nearly every week.

"This job is a life changer and will make me a millionaire all on my own without family money," she said, looking up with her wide light brown eyes. "You know I can't turn down this job now," she said.

"I think that was Thane's intention." Jake noticed she didn't have the look that his usual dates possessed. Except now that he was paying close attention, she did have thickly lashed, big light brown eyes, very smooth skin and full rosy lips. She wore no jewelry or makeup. His gaze flicked over her loose-fitting black cotton shirt and black slacks. The shirt hung to her hips, hiding her waist. So why was there some chemistry between them that kept the air around them electric? He was certain she felt it as much as he did.

"I can't believe this. Why would he give me a check this size? Why would he do this at all? There are others in this business who are successful."

"Thane was wealthy. He didn't want to leave loose ends and that meant hiring us. To pay that much, he obviously thought you're the best person for the job. Either that or he was hell-bent to try to put an end to the feud and having a Ralston and a Kincaid stay together on a ranch and work together is a start."

"Oh, yes, it is. This is like a dream," she said, looking down at the check again as if she still couldn't believe it. "I wasn't going to take this job. I didn't think there would be any way you could persuade me to accept your offer. There is a way and Thane found it. There are too many good things I can do with this money, plus help my own career along. I have to tell you, yes, I'll take the job."

Sitting back in his chair, he smiled at her, wondering how well they would work together. "Good. I want to do as much as I can to keep my promises to him. You get a million. I get another ranch, a chunk of West Texas—all to take care of an old house, private belongings that he didn't want to fall into the wrong hands and, at the same time, we'll at least be the first blow against the feud. Hopefully, when others see us work together and live under the same roof, they will lighten up about the feud."

"I hope my brothers don't cause any problems. They aren't going to like this. And neither will a lot of my relatives."

"This is a working ranch and from what Thane told me in the past, he has plenty of security, plus the cowboys and staff who live there. You can warn your brothers." He sat back and crossed his legs again. "Thane took very good care of things, but he hadn't gotten around to dealing with the house and its contents when he went into the service. I want to get out there as soon as possible and get the job done. I plan to go look at the house this week. Do you want to come along?"

"Yes. I'd like to see what we're talking about."

"Today is Wednesday. I have appointments tomorrow. Friday morning I'm going to see Thane's parents. That'll be tough, but I practically grew up in his house. Mr. Warner spent hours with Thane and me. He taught me how to fly-fish, how to use a knife so I wouldn't cut off my fingers, how to rope a calf. He came to our ball games. I need to go see him."

"That's fine."

"So how about Friday afternoon to go to Thane's ranch? Then we can fly back to Dallas and I'll take you to dinner that evening." While she was not his type, he wanted to show his appreciation for her taking the job and allowing him to keep his promise to Thane. "I'll pick you up here and we'll fly to the ranch. We'll look the house over and decide when we can start."

"If you want, I can get the cleaning crew started early because I have someone I work with often and they're reliable. I also know a couple of painters who can get the house painted inside and outside if you'd like."

"I'd like that. In addition to appraising the contents, you can get the house in livable condition again. I'd rather not deal with the day-to-day restoration. I have a good contractor you can use, but feel free to use your own painters and decorators. Do as much as you can and bill me."

"Fine. I also have a landscape crew if we need it."

"That's perfect. Let me know about anything or anyone else you need. When Thane inherited the ranch, it was actually a working ranch. Thane hired a guy to run it and get it in shape. Thane told me there's a bunkhouse, a kitchen and a dining area for the cowboys, a cook and an office near the bunkhouse. There are cattle, but not as many as there will be. And of course, there's the main house, which is a three-story frame house. Thane intended to come home and go through the house to decide what to do with things. When he was home before going to Afghanistan, neither he nor Vivian ever got around to it. As I understand it, the caretaker lives in a guesthouse close to the main house. I hope to keep everyone Thane hired. You oversee everything you can and put it on my bill. I'll deal with the men, the cattle and the horses, and my contractor."

She nodded.

"Emily, this is a job that neither of us wants to do, but it's worth our while to do it. You get to become a millionaire and I get a ranch. For that we can put up with some things we hadn't wanted to." He looked into her big brown eyes and was struck by a question out of the blue. What would it be like to kiss her?

The question startled him. What was it about her that made him wonder about kisses? She wasn't his type. She was practical, business-minded. But each time he looked at her, there was that wild undercurrent of awareness that he couldn't figure out. Each time it happened, she looked as startled as he felt, and he was certain it was not something that she wanted to have happen and not something that happened often to her. It didn't with him—not to this extent. Especially when it wasn't some gorgeous woman who flirted and wanted to stir up a reaction from him.

If they were going to live in the same house, he didn't want to have any kind of sizzling reaction to Emily.

So why couldn't he stop imagining that thick long blond hair, which was now tied behind her head with a yellow scarf, untied and falling over her shoulders? Or splayed against his naked chest? The minute those visions played out in his mind's eye, he tried to think of something else. Unsuccessfully.

When she stood, he came to his feet at once, his gaze flicking over her swiftly. "I suppose we're through now," she said.

"We are for today." He held out his hand, half doing it to be polite because they would be working closely together and living in the same house for a while. But the minute her hand touched his, he felt the same startling awareness of the contact and saw her blink and stare at him.

"I'll pick you up Friday afternoon," he said after clearing his throat hoarsely. "I'll call first." He looked her over again. "It's been…interesting. This is the longest I've ever had a polite conversation with a Kincaid."

She smiled slightly. "You're long overdue then. We really don't bite and are quite harmless."

"Your brothers aren't. Maybe that was back in high school." He followed her out of her office and down the hall to the front door. She didn't look the type for perfume, but there was some faint enticing scent that he didn't recognize. She was taller than most women he went out with, but still at least seven or eight inches shorter than he was. He opened the door and glanced back at her. "See you Friday."

"I'm still in a daze. I'm going to call Vivian. You're certain she knows about the check?"

"Absolutely."

When the door closed behind him, he let out his breath in a gush. *Keep your distance. And keep your hands off.* She was a Kincaid, and he expected some flak from at least one of her brothers. Some of the Kincaids and some of the Ralstons took this feud seriously and had a big dislike for the other family. Emily and he needed to move on this task and get through it. Yes, that's what he needed to do. Get the job done and forget her.

Dreading talking to Mr. and Mrs. Warner, Jake drove up to the familiar mansion spread over four acres of well-kept grounds with tall oaks. He'd spent hours here from the days when his mother dropped him off to play with Thane and on through high school when he and Thane would drive there after school at least three or four times a week. Thane had had a cook and there were snacks and a game room, a poolroom, an enclosed pool, a basketball court—Jake's family had had all of those at their house, as well, but Thane had had a tennis court at his and Jake hadn't. Sometimes a bunch of friends went with them, sometimes just Jake and Thane. Thane's dad was friendly and had always been interested in Jake and what he was doing at school.

Memories assailing him, Jake walked up the wide front steps to the porch with tall columns. A huge brass chandelier hung from the porch ceiling. He rang the chimes and a butler opened the door, smiling at Jake.

"Mr. Jake, welcome home."

"Thank you, Clyde."

"Come in. Mr. and Mrs. Warner are expecting

you. They're in the great room. We're so happy to see you."

"I'm glad to be here. It's good to see you. I wish Thane could be here with me," he said as they walked through a wide entryway where an elegant cherrywood table held a massive vase filled with white-and-purple orchids.

"So sad. They miss him. We all do, because he was a fine man." Clyde knocked on an open door and as they entered, he announced, "Mr. Jake is here."

Jake crossed the room to Celeste Warner, Thane's mother, who looked older and frailer than when he'd left. She was short and he leaned over to hug her lightly. As tears filled her eyes, she hugged him in return.

"I'm sorry he didn't make it home. We did what we could. It just wasn't enough," Jake said with a knot in his throat. Thane should have been here with him now.

Thane's father, Ben Warner, walked up, holding out his hand. Jake was surprised at how much Thane's dad had changed. His hair was whiter, he had more lines on his face than Jake remembered and he was thinner.

When they shook hands, Thane's dad slipped his arm around Jake and hugged him. "Thank God you made it home. It was bad losing Thane. I'm glad I didn't lose both of you," Ben said, and Jake hurt even more because this brought back painful memories. He hurt for Thane's parents, who had lost their oldest son, a son who had been unique and a super guy.

"Come sit and talk to us," Ben said, turning to sit in a leather recliner.

"Are you getting settled in now that you're back?" Celeste asked.

"Yes," Jake said. "I'm just glad to be home."

"We're glad you're here. What are your plans— a ranch or back to the family investment firm?" Thane's dad asked.

"Before I was in the army, I lived in Dallas and went to the investment office every day. Now I want to be a rancher. I'm ready for some open space and the challenges of ranch life. I'm still on the investment firm board and a couple of other boards, so I'll be in Dallas often. I'll be around." He settled back in the chair to talk to them. "I hear you are grandparents." Thane's sister, Camilla, had a seventeen-month-old.

"Yes, here's Ethan's picture. He's the image of his daddy," Ben said, handing a framed picture to Jake.

Jake looked at the little boy with his mop of black curls. "He does look like his dad." Jake knew his dad well. Noah Grant was one of the rangers he'd served with, and one of the buddies who had made promises to Thane. Noah had been charged with bringing important packages to Thane's sister and his nephew, and in the process he reignited his romance with Camilla and came face-to-face with the son he never knew he had.

Ben's eyes softened as he took back the photo. "Camilla and Noah seem so happy and so is their little Ethan. We see them often."

"Where are Logan and Mason?" he asked about Thane's younger brothers.

"Logan is president of our drilling company. Mason has taken over for me at the bank. They don't live far from us and you'll probably see them when you're in Dallas. Both are single."

After about twenty minutes Jake stood and said he had an appointment and needed to go. It took another ten minutes to tell Thane's mother goodbye and Thane's dad left with him, strolling back through the mansion, across the stone floor of the entryway and out to the front porch.

Jake turned to shake his hand. To his surprise, Ben hugged him again and stepped away. "I'm so relieved you made it home."

"Thank you, sir. I'm sorry Thane didn't. We all did what we could for him."

"I know you did," Ben said and wiped his eyes. He placed his hand on Jake's shoulder. "Come see us sometimes. Please keep in touch. You're family to us. You're another son, Jake. You always have been."

"Thank you, sir. That means a lot to me. You're the one who's been a real dad to me. I'm sorry for your loss and I'll keep in touch," he said, thinking of Thane. "We all miss him."

When he closed his car door and drove down the long drive, he let out his breath. He was glad the visit was over. Most of the time he could cope with the loss of his friend, but every once in a while he was overwhelmed with that pain he had felt when Thane died. He was surprised how Thane's dad had hugged him and wanted him to come back, but then he'd always been surprised by Ben's interest in him.

He made a mental note to try to see the Warners at least once a month for the next few months. Time would ease their pain, but for now he'd try to visit often. They had Noah and Camilla, the new grandchild, plus their other two sons, and they would help, but he knew the Warners would always miss Thane.

Friday afternoon, when a sleek black sports car stopped at Emily's store and office, she hurried out. She had dressed in practical sneakers, jeans and a white sweatshirt. Her clothes hid her figure and her hair was in one long braid down her back. She wanted to keep things businesslike with Jake. She hadn't understood the chemistry that smoldered between them when they'd met, but she hoped it was gone. While he was to-die-for handsome, she didn't want any kind of attraction. She had to do this job and work for him. He was her boss now, but she didn't want it to go beyond a boss-employee relationship.

That sentiment fizzled the moment he stepped out of the car. In jeans, boots, a white dress shirt open at the throat and a black Western hat, he was breathtakingly sexy. As she walked out to meet him, Jake didn't offer to shake her hand as he had the day they met, and she wondered what that implied.

"Ready and eager to go?" he asked, smiling, making her pulse jump with the irresistible curve of his lips.

"Yes. I like old things, antiques, so I'm curious what we'll find."

"I can't even guess. It may be a house filled with trash. We'll see."

As they drove away from her Dallas office, he watched traffic. "Did you tell your family what you're doing?"

"Not yet," she replied cheerfully. "That will be like dropping a bomb. I'm waiting for Sunday dinner when we all get together at my parents' house. I think you'll know when I've told them."

"Will I need a bodyguard?" he asked, smiling again, another dazzling grin that changed her heart rate.

"You better not need one." She thought for a

second, then told him, "Doug will be the worst. I'll have a private talk with him. He's calmed down a little since he got married."

"I know your brothers and I'm not worried. Your oldest brother and I didn't have the best relationship in school. He isn't going to be happy to know you're working for me."

"No, Doug won't, but Thane's gift to me is going to go a long ways toward smoothing things over. That's a lot of money. Besides, I'll make it clear that you and I will be together because of business. I'll be working for you, and my brothers know they better leave me alone to run my business the way I see fit."

"As I said, I think that's what Thane intended."

Jake drove to the airport, where his private plane waited. It was a quick flight to a landing strip at Flat Hill, Texas, a small Texas town with a wide main street, a grocery, a hardware store, a bank, a café and a bar. Jake had a new pickup waiting and he held the door for her.

As she stepped past him, she caught a whiff of his aftershave, so slight, but it heightened his appeal.

She slid into the passenger seat and he closed the door. When he circled the pickup, her gaze ran over his broad shoulders and his narrow waist. She hoped they didn't work too closely together. Life would be easier if they didn't, because no matter what she did she couldn't shake her awareness of him. On the plane, she'd occasionally looked up and caught him staring at her, desire blatant in his dark eyes. When their gazes met, it was as if they had made physical contact. She couldn't understand the chemistry between them, but it was still going strong.

She had to remember Jake was a playboy. He didn't want to marry anytime soon—maybe ever. He didn't want a family. He had women in his life but he didn't keep them around long. He was all the things she wouldn't want in a man in her life. And he wasn't anything like the men in her family.

So why was she aware of his very presence from the second he slid into the driver's seat and closed his door?

It was three o'clock when they turned beneath a metal arch that read Long L.

"Do you know who the Long L was named after?" she asked and Jake shook his head.

"No, one of the early day Warners, I suppose." As he drove along a narrow dirt trail that almost disappeared in weeds, high grass and cacti, her curiosity grew. In minutes, she could see a large three-story weathered house on a rise. Tall oaks were on either side of the house, ancient trees that had long spreading limbs.

"That's not what I'd expected," she said, gazing at the house.

"It's impressive," Jake said. "According to Thane, it was built in 1890."

"If it's lasted well over a century, it must be well-built." The house looked Victorian, with one large turret on the second floor, a dormer on the third floor and three balconies on the second floor, all with fancy balustrades like the porch. "I think I'm going to love working on this old house."

"I'll remember to avoid taking you to my condo with a very contemporary kitchen."

She smiled at him. "I like contemporary, too. Antiques are my first love, though."

"This ranch house looks more elaborate than I'd expected," he said, peering at it through the windshield.

"And more charming, because I can imagine how it will look with a new coat of paint and all fixed up," she said.

"I've never been on this ranch before," Jake said. "Thane's grandmother died first and his family didn't like their grandfather, so we didn't spend any time out here. No telling what we'll find. Thane said his great-great-grandfather was a horse thief and a bank robber and did plenty the family didn't talk about."

As Jake spoke of the ranch's history, Emily couldn't help but feel eager to get to work. She hadn't wanted this job, but she had gotten into the antiques-and-appraisal business because she loved old things, and as she looked at the large ranch home that was over a hundred years old, she couldn't keep from being curious and excited about what they would find in it. The prospect of living in it, working constantly with Jake, added to the excitement bubbling inside her.

"We're not going to find any bodies, are we?"

Jake laughed as he shook his head. "Nope. At least, I hope not. As far as I know, Thane's grandfather was only a gambler. He must have been good at it to hang on to this ranch. That's an imposing-looking house. I figured we'd find something that should be leveled. That's what Thane suggested and I think what he intended to do. We'll have to see what it's like inside, but if it's solid, I'm not tearing it down."

"Tearing it down would be a real loss," she agreed. "I can't believe I'm going to live in that for the next few weeks."

"Count on weeks. I'm guessing the inside is filled with stuff, from what Thane indicated. Years of stuff. If so, it'll take time to go through it." They drove over rocks and through a stream that was only a trickle.

"Someone is there. See that pickup by the oak?" she asked, pointing ahead.

"That's the caretaker, who's also in charge of security. Rum McCloud. I don't know whether Rum is a nickname or his real name. I notified him that we were coming."

Standing in the shade, a lanky man in a plaid long-sleeve Western shirt, jeans, boots and a broad-brimmed hat waited with his hands on his hips. They parked and Jake went around to open the door for Emily, but she stepped out quickly.

Jake walked up to Rum and held out his hand. "I'm Jake Ralston and this is Emily Kincaid."

"Howdy, folks. Rum McCloud. Welcome to the Long L. Here's two house keys and my card with my phone number and email address. Anything I can do for you, just let me know. You can call or text." Rum aso handed Jake three key rings, which he assumed were for locks inside the house.

"Thanks. We'll go look at it. We plan to stay in the house to get stuff sorted and out of it. I'll let you know, Rum, what we end up doing."

"Fine. We can send dinner up from the big kitchen for you. My crew will still be around 24/7. We watch this place."

He looked over his shoulder at the house. "The place needs repairs, but it's time and weather that's taken a toll. We keep vandals, kids and drifters away from here. After his grandfather died, Mr. Warner came and looked at the place, locked it up and left and never came back. Inside that house is just like his grandfather left it. I'm sorry about Thane. He was a fine man."

"Yes, he was. We became friends too far back to remember. I told you on the phone—I intend to keep this ranch, raise cattle and keep you and the other men who are here now. You can pass the word on that."

"Glad to hear that. I'll pass it along. Everyone is wondering about the future. Now I can tell them they still have a job."

"Yes, you can. The only quick changes will be to this house. We're not staying tonight. We're only here to take a look inside the house. I'll let you know when we'll be back and when we'll stay to go through stuff. Hopefully, we'll start next week," he said, glancing at Emily, and she nodded.

"I can do that," she said, mentally going through her business calendar. Next week would fit her schedule nicely, and she was looking forward to getting her hands on the antiques.

There was only one thing she was still fretting over. Living out here with Jake Ralston.

Emily said goodbye to Rum and was aware of Jake beside her as they walked to the front steps.

"This was a grand old house in its day," Jake said. He paused at the foot of the steps to look up at the house.

"I think it's still a wonderful house," she said and he looked down at her and smiled.

"Why do I think that you are a definite optimist?"

She shrugged. "I like the house and I see the good side of keeping it. Cleaned up and freshly painted, it could be charming. I've already sent a text to my assistant and she's getting a cleaning crew lined up for tomorrow."

"We'll see what my contractor says. He knows a lot about houses."

After crossing the porch, Jake unlocked the oversize door, which swung open. The entryway had a marble floor with a stone fountain that had no water. The fountain was centered in a shallow circular marble pool, also dry and with a thick layer of dust. Above that, the ceiling soared to the second floor with a dust-and-cobweb-covered chandelier hanging high above the empty fountain. She couldn't judge the condition of the furnishings, since they were all covered with sheets.

"I never was here with Thane. He told me he hated coming here. He said his grandfather didn't take care of it and it was a depressing mess. I see what he meant if this was the way the old man lived."

Emily took pictures with her phone. "I'm sending these to Leslie so she'll have an idea what this cleaning job is going to entail."

They walked around the empty fountain and a wide dark hallway stretched ahead of them.

Nearby, two sweeping staircases led to the second floor and a high ceiling above it.

He started walking down the dark hallway and paused. "What a mess this is," he said, pointing at the packing boxes that stood in the hall and in the rooms they peeked into. Papers littered the floors, cobwebs were growing in corners and windows were covered with grime on the outside. Inside, dust coated everything. They entered another room filled with shelves and books and found the same situation. A desk was covered with notebooks. Along one wall were locked cabinets with wooden doors. Jake looked at the three key rings he'd been given.

"I think there should be a key here for each of these cabinets." He ran his hand over a dusty cabinet door. "From the looks of these, I'd guess they hold guns."

"Guns? Maybe." She leaned closer to look, glancing again at the lock. "You have maybe forty keys on those rings."

"There are numbers on them. This is ring number one," he said, holding a ring with keys of various sizes and shapes. "We can try these next week after they get the dirt and cobwebs out of here."

"You can just walk away and not try to get in and see what's inside?" she asked.

He turned to focus on her. "Yes, I can." He

looked amused. "You can't? Be my guest, then," he said, holding out the three key rings.

"You really don't care?"

"No, I don't. You're hired to help me clear this stuff out, remember?"

"You go look at more rooms and I'll try the keys. I'm too curious to wait. What's in here? A hidden bar? Rare books? Family albums? Whatever it is, there's a lot of it," she said, looking at the cabinets covering one wall.

"Here," he said, taking her hand in his and placing the key rings in it. The moment he took her hand, everything changed. She forgot the keys, cabinets, even the house. That fiery awareness flared again and she knew he felt it, too, because his chest expanded as he inhaled while he flicked a questioning look at her and continued holding her hand.

"Does that happen to you with every guy you meet?" he asked quietly and her heart thudded.

She didn't need to ask what he was talking about. She shook her head. "No," she whispered. "Not ever. I figured it's something you always have happen, though. You do have a reputation for attracting the ladies." Her heart drummed and she had a prickling awareness of him, of his hand still holding hers as he ran his thumb so lightly back and forth over her knuckles.

"It happens sometimes, but not quite like this,"

he replied. "And never with someone I work with. Not ever. You're unique in my life, Emily," he said and she shook her head.

"I think I'll forget looking in the cabinets this afternoon," she said, giving him back the keys and yanking her hand away from his, eager to put some distance between them. "Let's make a quick tour of this floor. I'll take the other side of the hall and you do this side and we'll meet at the other end of the house." She didn't want to have a reaction to him and she couldn't allow the moment to get personal. She had to work with him for a few weeks at least. When they got the place cleaned up, they would stay here, some nights just the two of them. She didn't want to have a breathtaking, instant, heart-racing reaction to him every time their hands brushed.

She felt ridiculous and wished she could have passed off her response as nothing, but she couldn't. She had never had reactions like that to a man she didn't know. And she didn't want to start with Jake. He was a Ralston. The last person she wanted to have a fiery attraction to.

She hurried away, crossing the hall to a great room that held a huge marble fireplace. Here again, the furniture was covered with sheets. From what he'd told her, she had expected to find a wreck of a house. Instead, it looked solid and soundly built.

She entered a ballroom-sized dining room with

a huge table covered by canvas that draped over the chairs. She lifted a corner and looked at an elaborately carved table and chairs with faded antique satin striped upholstery. She wasn't particularly happy to see some fine furniture because it meant working with him longer. If it had all been ruined and ready to dispose of, the job would have been over quickly.

She left the dining room and moved to a large kitchen. The kitchen was the room that needed to be replaced. Everything was old, with out-of-date appliances and a chipped, rusted sink, but the room itself was big and could be updated easily. The real question might turn out to be how important the house was to Jake. What did he ultimately want since this was now his ranch?

A sunroom stretched across the back of the house. There she found what she had expected throughout the house—worn, broken chairs, overturned tables, nothing worth saving. The whole room needed to be gutted and the furniture dumped.

When Emily met Jake in the hall, he shook his head. "This is going to take some work. I don't think we need to look upstairs. There's enough here to know we have a job ahead of us. I went through the library, the study that's under years of dust and had more locked cabinets. I went through an office with locked files, a locked desk, a locked closet. One good thing—there are three big downstairs bedrooms, each with its own bath. Can you get started right away on getting new furniture for two of those bedrooms and something for the windows? It can all be temporary, just so we have a clean place to stay."

"Yes, I will."

"I want an office I can work in with a desk, a file cabinet, a long table and a place for three computers and screens. You'll need an office, too, so you'll have to furnish it however you like. Get a sofa and a couple of chairs and about four big-screen televisions, so we have one in each room we'll be living in."

She took out her tablet and jotted notes while he talked.

"We'll have meals sent up from the cook and maybe work out some kind of delivery from that little café in Flat Hill, so we'll need a table where we can eat. Or maybe we can use the big table in the dining room. I peeked into that kitchen. It's got to go. It's the biggest disaster in the house so far."

"I agree." As she finished jotting notes, she was only half thinking about her writing. She was aware of Jake standing inches away.

"I'll give you a credit card for the furniture. Just have the pieces sent out here. I'll tell Rum."

"Sure. I'll be glad to. Give me a limit you want to spend."

"No limit. Use your judgment. Just get something several notches above nice. I want to be comfortable and frankly, I'm not worried about the cost. I want comfort and a place I don't mind living in."

She nodded. "I'll get everything with the agreement they have to take it back if it doesn't suit you. I can send you pictures—"

"No," he interrupted, shaking his head and looking amused. "I don't want to make furniture decisions. I don't care. You do it and put it on my bill."

"It really might help if we could go by your Dallas home and I can see what style of furniture you like. Would that be possible?" she asked, aware of inviting herself to his Dallas home.

"Sure, we can. I have a condo. I think we might as well go back to Dallas now. I don't want to work in this dirt and dust. You get that cleaning crew out here and some furniture bought and delivered, and we'll come back. We can make plans on the plane."

"Before we go, I need to get the measurements of where I'm putting furniture so I'll have an idea about how much room I'll have."

"Sure. I'll help."

All the time she walked with him down the wide hall, she couldn't stop the intense awareness of him so close beside her.

"This may be a big job," she said, trying to focus on the job instead of the man. While she thought about the amount of work this house might demand, she couldn't keep from worrying about working side by side with Jake. She was already too aware of him walking close beside her. Would they continue to have that chemistry bubbling between them?

They walked into the first bedroom and she got out her metal tape measure. Jake intended to have bedroom suites built upstairs, but for the time being they'd be staying in these first-floor rooms.

He held out his hand. "Give me the end of the tape." She did and he walked to the corner while she wrote down the measurement.

She pressed the button for the tape to roll up and then Jake took it from her to measure the next wall. Within minutes they had two bedrooms done and moved on to measure the library and the study. As they worked together, their hands brushed lightly, just feathery touches, yet she was intensely aware of each contact. How could she not be, when each of them fanned the flames of desire burning inside her? More than anything she wanted to finish and head home. She snapped shut her measuring tape. "There. It's done—" She turned and bumped into him. He caught her upper arms to steady her but didn't let her go. They stood there, looking into each other's eyes, and she couldn't move.

While longing intensified, her gaze lowered to

his mouth. Seconds passed and then she looked up at him again.

He was going to kiss her.

She knew that with every fiber of her being. Just as she knew she should stop him. But her breath wouldn't come and her heart thudded violently as he slipped his arm around her waist and leaned down. Closer. And closer.

And with his lips a breath away, caution was the last thing on her mind.

Three

His mouth settled on hers, opening hers, his tongue going deep. His kiss was electrifying, intoxicating, addicting, making her want him to do nothing but kiss her the rest of the day and never stop. He pulled her more tightly against him, crushing her against his rock-hard muscled chest as he wrapped both arms around her, and she was lost, spiraling down into need and desire, wanting him desperately.

His tongue stroked hers, tantalizing and melting her, yet making her tremble, respond and want him. Without even being aware of it, she wrapped her arm around his neck and thrust her hips against him, feeling his arousal as he held her tightly and they continued to kiss.

His kiss consumed her, ignited desire and made her world spin away to a place where logic no longer existed. Only Jake and his hard body and hot lips. She wanted nothing but his kiss, his touch, and she wanted him to never stop. She clung to him and kissed him in return, holding him and knowing her world had shifted and changed.

Her pleasure was so intense, she thought she would faint, yet she couldn't allow it. She wanted every second of his kiss, every sensation. She tingled all over, consumed with desire—all because of his mouth on hers. She had never been kissed like this, never reacted to a kiss with so much desperate hunger, a longing for more of him. But Jake's kiss made her want his hands, his mouth all over her. Made her want to join their bodies together, right there and now in this dusty house.

From somewhere in the depths of longing came the voice of caution and reason, but she ignored it as she ran her hand over his broad shoulder, down his back to his waist. She held him tightly and kissed him in return, pouring herself into a kiss that she dimly realized she would never forget.

He caressed her nape and she moaned softly with pleasure, never wanting to step out of the haven of his arms. How could he do this to her with a kiss?

A Ralston man, at that.

Her boss.

The reality of who this man was slowly crept past the ecstasy induced by his kiss. The two factions warred in her head as Jake's hand drifted down her back and over her bottom, pulling her impossibly closer. Oh, what she wouldn't give to shed her clothes and feel his skin against hers, let him do all the things his kiss was promising. Let him—

As reality won the war, the insanity of what she was doing slammed into her. She wiggled away and gasped for breath as if she had run a marathon, opening her eyes and looking up at him.

He was breathing as heavily as she was, looking at her with hooded eyes, his mouth red from their kiss.

"That kiss never happened," she somehow managed to whisper. "We—we have to go back to where we were so we can work together."

He placed his hand so lightly on her neck, slipping his hand around to caress her nape and sending a thrill sizzling in the wake of his touch. "Darlin', there is no way in this lifetime I can forget that kiss and say it never happened." His voice was husky, his eyes intense, as if he had never seen her before the past ten minutes.

"You have to forget our kiss if you want us—" she paused to get her breath; she was still gasping for air, still tingling all over, still wanting to wrap her arms around him, place her mouth on his and kiss him the rest of the day and night "—if you want us to be able to work together for the next few weeks. I don't want to give back Thane's check or turn down this job, but kisses and sex can't go with working together."

He reached out for her and opened his mouth as if he were going to argue the point, but she drew a shaky breath and continued, "We have to back off or I can't take this job." She ran a hand over her lips and down her throat, as if trying to wipe away a kiss she knew she'd never forget. "I know I wanted that kiss as much as you, but I'm trying to do what I know is sensible."

He stood staring at her and then he rubbed the back of his neck. "Yeah. I know you're right. We've got tasks to do and I don't want to let Thane down. Even though he's gone, I made promises and I intend to keep them to the best of my ability. And I don't want to hurt you in any way. I want you to know I've never done this before. Never crossed the line with an employee. Never dated one, flirted with one or kissed one…until you."

"I'm as responsible as you, Jake. But like I said, from this moment forward we forget it happened." She shook her head. "Neither of us wanted that kiss to happen. It was an anomaly, that's all. I haven't been out with anyone in a while and you've been overseas in the army. That's all it was. You'll get back into your life and I'll keep socializing with my friends and we'll forget this. It won't happen again," she whispered and wondered when she'd actually start believing what she was saying. "Besides, I'm not your type and you're not my type."

He nodded. "We've got a business agreement and I don't think sex and business mix well. You're correct and logical, and it would be smart to stick to business. That's not impossible to do," he said.

She had never spent any time with Jake Ralston, but for some reason she doubted the sincerity in his words. His eyes flittered and his speech was halting, as if he was trying to convince himself of what he was promising.

And her? She hoped she could live up to her speech. She knew she couldn't forget his kiss ever. In fact, she wanted to walk right back into his arms even now, but she wasn't going to because that would lead her down a rocky path straight to heartbreak. It would be too easy to fall in love with him—the deep, forever kind of love that would hurt badly when he said goodbye. And he would definitely say goodbye, just as he'd done to countless women before her.

The man may be handsome and exciting and loaded with sex appeal, and she may have never been kissed like that before, but it was over. Someday another man would come along who could make her forget Jake's kisses.

For now, she needed to get this job done as soon as possible and she needed to work without being anywhere near him.

Despite her internal pep talk, a hot awareness of him curled up inside her as she picked up her tablet with the written measurements. Moments ago she had dropped it and her stylus along with her wits. Right now, she needed to get some fresh air and get away from the magnetism of Jake Ralston.

"I'm ready to go back to Dallas," she said. "We've done what we could today. This is going to be a big job," she repeated, flipping the switch to business mode.

"I agree. You'll get the cleaning crew—that's the first step before moving furniture in and before we come out here to work. For now, let's get back to Dallas and have a steak dinner and forget this."

"You're sure you want to be seen in public with a Kincaid? Word travels fast, you know. You don't have to take me to dinner."

"After this grungy mess, we should have a steak dinner. As far as being seen together tonight, Dallas is big. I belong to a club and there are no Kincaids who are members. We should have a quiet evening. Remember, Thane had hopes we'd bring about the end of the Ralston-Kincaid feud. So if we're seen together, that may be a good thing."

Emily knew she should not have accepted the dinner invitation, but it sounded wonderful in the first place and in the second, she didn't want him to think her refusal had anything to do with their kiss. So she smiled and nodded. "Sounds grand. Let's go."

He sent a text to Rum and when they walked out on the porch, they saw his pickup approaching. Jake went down the steps to meet Rum and she followed, noticing Jake didn't take her arm.

He kept a distance between them as they flew home. He was friendly and polite, though a little more reserved and standoffish, which suited her. She didn't want any lingering sparks between them to ignite into fires. She tried to keep her thoughts about their kiss locked away, not wanting to think about how wonderful it had felt or how wantonly she had reacted. Instead, she focused on her family, namely how she was going to deal with their reaction when she announced the gift from Thane and the job she had agreed to do. Doug and Lucas, especially, would not be happy over her job, but the money should make up for that.

The short flight went quickly and Jake drove her home so she could change and get ready when he returned to get her for dinner. He let her out at her house and waited until she opened the door before he drove away. She stepped inside and went to shower, pausing in her room and letting out her breath. His kiss had been dazzling, unforgettable. Just remembering being in Jake's arms and kissing him made her hot, tingling, wanting him and his kisses and his hands all over her again.

"Business," she whispered, closing her eyes. She opened them instantly because when she closed her eyes, memories enveloped her. Memories of thrilling sensations, of sexy longings, of the kiss of a lifetime.

"Stick to business," she whispered while she thought about his body pressed against hers. It was going to be incredibly difficult to stick to business with him, but she had to do so or risk a broken heart that might not ever mend.

How long would it take to forget their kiss?

A lifetime was her first answer.

No, she couldn't accept that response. She had to forget it. There was no hope for her and Jake Ralston together. A man like him would never ever fall in love with a woman like her. And she wouldn't even like it if he did. From what she knew of his family, he wouldn't fit into her family even if he wanted to, or if she wanted him to. He had already said he didn't get along with Doug or Lucas. And Will liked everyone except Ralstons.

She shook her head. It was hopeless. Perseverating on Jake would only lead to trouble and heartbreak.

Stepping into the shower, she washed away

the memories of his kiss. Or at least she tried to. By the time she toweled herself dry, she had a plan. She needed to keep her hair braided, forego makeup, stop using any perfume, dress plainly. Anything to make her less noticeable to him. That would work to keep their palpable attraction at bay.

Or was she fooling herself?

It took ten minutes to select a plain black dress with a round collar, long sleeves and a belted waist. It was simple, subdued and she wouldn't draw attention, but it would be fine for a dinner club. She went against her game plan and let her hair fall freely around her face.

With some time to spare, she sat down and made notes of potential questions for Jake. Questions about the job as well as safe topics they could discuss if desire reared its head during dinner. She would be glad when the evening was over because since their kiss, she had been on edge the rest of the time she was with him. She was too aware of him, of the sparks popping between them, of desire that she tried to bank. He was a handsome, sexy, appealing man who, she was sure, had left a trail of broken hearts behind. He had a reputation for loving women and parties and she didn't fit into that lifestyle at all. Now if she could only remember that, the evening would go well.

When she heard a car, she looked out the window to see Jake get out and stride up her walk.

He wore a dark navy suit, black boots and a black Stetson, and he looked incredibly handsome. Soon he would stride back out of her life—a fact she should keep in mind tonight and whenever she was with him. If only she could keep the evening on a friendly yet businesslike basis, then their relationship could get back on an even keel.

When her doorbell rang, she picked up her purse and opened the door, realizing the futility of her pep talk when she felt her racing pulse.

All the time he showered and dressed, Jake promised himself that while he was going to dinner tonight with Emily, she was as off-limits as if she were married. Their kiss today had been exactly what he had intended to avoid. When they'd bumped into each other and he'd looked into her eyes, he'd wanted her with all his being. And she'd wanted his kiss just as badly. There had been no reluctance or hesitation on her part. And that kiss was the sexiest, hottest kiss he had ever experienced. How could she get that kind of reaction out of him when she definitely wasn't his type?

There—he'd admitted it to himself. He had been stunned, set ablaze with desire, wanting to take her home to bed with him. Actually, that kiss had made him want to have sex with her right then in that dusty old house. If she had wanted sex, he wouldn't have cared about the dust. She made him lose every shred of common sense. Why, of all the gorgeous, sexy, eager women he had dated and known, did the one who melted him down have to be a Kincaid—sworn enemies of the Ralstons for over a century.

Make friends with them...

Thane's words echoed in his head. Friends, he repeated to himself. Seducing Emily was not what his friend had had in mind.

He could do that. He knew how to control his libido. He knew how to control a lot of things, so why had he lost it with a plain-Jane employee who really didn't want to be with him? Who was all wrong for him.

He knew that much about her, just by knowing her family. They were family people. Not multiple-marriage people like his family. She didn't approve of him. What shook him so badly, though, was that in spite of all these reasons, his kiss with Emily had been the best of his life—and that was a real shock because he had kissed some very kissable women. Dazzling, sexy beauties by any man's standards. He had thought he'd experienced kisses as sexy as possible. But he had been wrong.

"Dammit," he said aloud, looking around him. For an instant he had forgotten where he was and what he was doing, so lost was he in memories of Emily's kiss. One more thing that no other woman had ever done.

He turned onto her drive and walked to her door to ring the bell. Instantly, the door swung open and his heart thudded. She wore a black dress and while it didn't cling tightly to her figure, it fit close enough to reveal her tiny waist and curves that he could remember holding tightly against him that afternoon. She was attractive and she had a perfect figure, with those enticing soft curves. In a glance, he noticed everything about her, from her black pumps with high heels to her blond hair falling around her face. It looked soft and silky, curling slightly on her shoulders, and she would turn heads tonight. He felt as if he were sinking into quicksand. He didn't want to be attracted to her. The woman he faced now—instead of being an employee and a business acquaintance—had become the sexiest, most desirable woman he had ever known simply because they'd kissed. Only, there wasn't one simple thing about that sizzling kiss.

"Ready to go?" he asked.

"Yes, I am." She stepped out and he heard the door lock when she closed it. He was glad she hadn't invited him inside.

"I've heard back from my friend about cleaning and she can have three crews on your ranch on Wednesday. How's that?" she asked as they strolled to his car.

"Excellent. I'll let Rum know and he can let them inside."

Jake held the car door for her and she slid onto the passenger seat. When she climbed in and sat down, her short skirt revealed more of her legs, gorgeous long legs that stirred desire even as he knew his response was not good news.

When he slid behind the wheel, he was acutely aware of her beside him.

"Is there a guy in your life who might not want you working on the Long L?" he asked her.

"Oh, yes, three of them," she replied and he gave her a startled glance. "My brothers, Doug, Lucas and Will," she answered, smiling. "Will is younger and he won't feel as strongly as Doug and Lucas. I'll deal with them. Otherwise, there's no other guy to care."

"You act as if that's an impossibility," he said, smiling at her.

"Not impossible, but there's no one. My family is close and we're together a lot, which is intimidating to some guys."

"I can see that. Well, my family is scattered to hell and gone. We don't get together and some of them don't even speak to each other. That's more my mom's generation and her exes'."

"This dinner is nice of you, but in hindsight, we probably should have grabbed a burger somewhere away from Dallas. I can't imagine we won't encounter someone who will be shocked to see us together. My brothers are all over the place. I'm always running into them."

"By Sunday, your family will know we're going to work together so it really won't matter if they find out tonight. I think this is part of what Thane wanted—for the Ralstons and the Kincaids to know we're working together and that we can get along."

"You seem to know my family, but I don't know yours. Don't you have a sister who is a popular country singer?"

"Yes, a half sister. My mother has had four husbands. Brent Ralston was the first and they had two sons and a daughter. They had my older brothers Grayson and Clay. Grayson has had two wives and is currently divorced. He has two kids by his first wife, one by the second wife. Clay is also divorced. He has one child. Next, I have a sister, Eva Ralston, who is two years older than I am. She's divorced and lives in Chicago and has no kids. My brothers have discouraged marriage for Eva and me. They are very much against it after their bitter divorces. So you can see we're not good marriage material."

"Your family and my family are poles apart. We're together constantly. My sister, Andrea, and her husband, James, are very happily married with two cute kids. Doug and Lydia are happily married and so are my folks."

"My dad was the second husband, another Ralston. Dwight was a cousin of the first Ralston husband, which caused rifts among some of the clan. You can imagine our family reunions are interesting. A whole different world from you and your family." He shrugged. "That was my mom's shortest marriage. Dwight Ralston and Mom divorced when I was just a year old. He lives in Houston and I barely know him. After he was gone, then came two more stepdads.

"With Salvo Giancola—we called him 'Papa Sal'—my mother had a boy, Ray, and then a girl, Gina. Gina is the country singer. Papa Sal tried to be a good dad, but he liked the ladies and my mom divorced him. When he left, Ray went with him and Gina stayed with Mom. The fourth and current husband is Harry Willingham and I finished growing up with Harry as a dad, but he wasn't interested in kids."

"I'm still amazed your mother married two Ralston men," she said.

"My family surprises a lot of people."

"We're a traditional family," she said, and he could feel her gaze on him as he drove. "We're close and Mom and Dad have been married thirty-six years. We're together every weekend. My family gathers at our parents' house on Sunday evenings for dinner and several times a year we have big family get-togethers with all the local Kincaids invited."

"The fights would be on if we had big get-togethers like that. Mom had some bitter divorces and with two Ralston husbands it's touchy. That's part of why I don't want to marry and I don't want a family."

"I'm so sorry," she said, sounding so sad he had to smile.

"Don't be. It's my choice. I don't want a life like my mom or my dad and stepdads. I'm not close with my real dad at all."

"I'm so sorry," she repeated and he smiled.

"You sound as if I just announced I've decided to live alone on an island the rest of my life. I really don't feel sad about the choice I've made for my future. After watching my family, marriage doesn't look like such a hot deal to me."

"My goodness," she said, sounding more sad than ever and he knew she felt sorry for him, a reaction he'd never had from a woman before. Sure, plenty of times they weren't happy to hear him say he didn't intend to marry. There were times they obviously thought they could change his mind, and there were other times they felt the same as he did. But he hadn't ever encountered a woman who sounded as if he had a pitiful, disastrous future ahead of him.

After Jake parked, he took Emily's arm to walk inside to the lobby of the tall building, which housed the club. He placed a hand on her back and felt that same smoldering awareness of touching her and being close to her. Despite his vows earlier that day, desire rose in him. He wanted to stop and take her into his arms and kiss her. That was not what he wanted to feel, so he released her and just walked beside her.

"Oh, there's my brother," she said when they approached the center of the lobby. "I told you, I see someone in my family everywhere I go," she said, stepping in front of Jake. "Don't worry. I'll deal with him."

Jake looked over her head and recognized her second-oldest brother approaching them and looking ready for a fight. Jake stepped out from behind her and she stepped right back in front of him. "I'll take care of Lucas."

Jake laughed. "I'll talk to him. I'm not going to hide behind you and I'm not scared. I didn't come home after fighting in Afghanistan to get clobbered by your brother in a downtown lobby. It's not going to happen." She looked up at him as he grinned at her.

"I guess you're not afraid, but Lucas doesn't need to cause me trouble and this is sort of a family matter."

Jake watched Lucas Kincaid striding toward

him. With his blond hair, there was a family resemblance, but Lucas wore a scowl and his fists were clenched. After what he had gone through in the army, the whole thing was laughable, except Jake didn't want to fight with her brother. Especially when he was with Emily only for business reasons.

"Hi, Lucas," he said.

"Get away from my sister," Lucas snarled. His face was slightly red and his blue eyes sparked with anger.

She stepped between them quickly and poked her brother's shoulder with her finger. "Lucas, go home now. This is a business matter and not a social event, and I'll discuss it with the whole family when we're together because it concerns all of you."

Lucas's gaze narrowed and flicked to Jake and back to her. "Business?"

"Yes, and if you don't move on, you're going to regret this. You're interfering in my business dealings. Good night, Lucas." She turned to Jake. "Shall we go?"

Smiling, Jake nodded. "See you, Lucas." As they passed her brother, Jake fought the temptation to look over his shoulder.

"Don't worry, he won't jump you from behind. That announcement shocked him and he's probably watching us and trying to figure out what's going on."

"I'm not turning around to look."

"My brothers will leave you alone. I'll see to that."

He smiled and took her arm lightly to enter the elevator. "Thanks for the protection but I'm not worried about your brothers."

"I guess you're not," she said, her gaze running across his shoulders and making him draw a deep breath because she was studying him intently. "They can be so nice and so annoying," she said.

"That's family," he said, letting out his breath. "At least, it describes my family." He held her arm, aware he still had that instant, intense reaction to touching her. She stood close beside him and his gaze drifted over her. Her skin was smooth and warm, soft beneath his fingers. When she looked up, their gazes locked.

While his pulse jumped, his attention shifted to her rosy lips that were too appealing, too sexy. He clenched his fists to keep from putting his arm around her and pulling her closer for a kiss.

As if offering him a reprieve, the elevator stopped with a slight jerk and the door opened.

Jake inhaled deeply and released her as she turned to step out of the elevator. His heart raced and he couldn't understand the response she stirred in him just by standing beside him. If they'd been somewhere private, he would have kissed her— something he had intended to avoid doing again.

Fighting her brother in the lobby would have held fewer consequences than kissing her a second time. Today's kiss had already changed their whole business relationship before they'd even started working at the ranch. He felt as if he had lost common sense and good judgment. He couldn't understand the attraction or the effect she had on him. She didn't want to feel it any more than he did, so what happened when they got near each other?

He needed to pull his wits together and not touch her. He'd told himself that before, more than once. Had he made a big mistake in hiring her and asking her to work with him at the ranch as Thane had asked him to do? He thought of Thane and his promise to his dying friend and knew that, no matter how difficult it would be, he had to keep that vow.

As they entered the private restaurant for club members only, a tall balding maître d' greeted him.

"Good evening, Mr. Ralston. So glad to see you."

"Ted, this is Ms. Kincaid."

"I'm happy to meet you," he said, smiling at Emily and turning again to Jake. "Your table is ready." He picked up menus and led the way to a table in a quiet corner by a window with a view of Dallas against the setting sun. They had passed a piano player, who was playing quiet music in the background.

Jake held her chair and was aware of her hair brushing his fingers when she sat down. He walked around the table to sit facing her as their waiter appeared.

"I'll give you a moment to look over the menu. In the meantime, what would you like to drink?"

Jake ordered a bottle of champagne and glasses of water for them. As soon as they were alone, she raised her eyebrows as she looked at him. "Champagne?"

"Do you like champagne? I should have asked first."

"Yes, I like it, but what are you celebrating? Or are you just a champagne drinker?"

Smiling, he shook his head. "No, beer is my drink of choice. But tonight I'm celebrating that we're getting started on a job that needs to be done. I'm celebrating that you took the job and we'll clear out the house, so that I can keep my promise to Thane. And I'm celebrating that we'll make some sort of dent in the feud. In fact, we might have started making a change in the feud tonight."

"I really don't think that's possible." She smiled and his breath caught. Her smile was so contagious, so infectious that he felt it stir longings as it drew his attention to her rosy lips. He realized then that his champagne celebration might have been premature. He still didn't want to get involved with her, still knew she was not the woman for him, but he couldn't stop wanting to kiss her. How long would they be able to work together? Once they started living together at the ranch, would he be able to keep his distance from her?

Asking that question to himself, he had a sudden thought. Had Thane been trying to be a matchmaker with him the way he had with Mike and Vivian and with Noah and Camilla? Jake didn't think so. He thought Thane's big wish had been to end the feud between the Ralstons and the Kincaids; it would make running his ranch much easier for Mike Moretti since the Tumbling T was situated directly between properties belonging to the two feuding families.

Regardless of Thane's intentions, Jake realized that everything he had been determined to do to keep his relationship with Emily strictly business was crumbling by the hour. He reminded himself that she didn't want a personal relationship, either, and that they were a definite mismatch. He tried to focus on the menu instead of the woman across from him and settled on steak as he had originally planned. He had eaten here enough to know what he liked.

After the waiter brought their waters, Emily took a sip and leveled those beautiful brown eyes on him. "It occurred to me that I know so little about you. I mean, with us working together—"

she took another sip "—well, it might help to get acquainted."

"What do you want to know?"

"Well, how long are you home?"

"I'm the last one to come home of the three of us who made promises to Thane. I left Afghanistan in August and was discharged the last day of August. I haven't seen Noah Grant and Mike Moretti yet, but I intend to soon. For Mike and Noah, keeping those promises changed their lives. If the Ralston-Kincaid feud ends, that will be a life changer for a lot of us."

"A change for the better. It seems ridiculous when you stop to think about it. We might cause the younger Kincaids and Ralstons to view the feud differently and see that we can have peace, but I don't think you can change the older ones."

"Honestly, I'll be surprised if anyone changes very much—except maybe the two of us," he said, smiling at her and getting another enticing smile in return.

"You're a rancher, but you have other interests, don't you? I've heard my dad say you're an investment broker."

"I was until I went into the army. I liked living in Dallas. I liked the city, the social life, the parties, the fun, the friends. But after being in the military, I'm ready for the ranch and now because of Thane,

I have two ranches. I have a ranch in the Hill Country and I love it there. That's where I want to live."

"I see pictures of you taken at parties and benefits. They're in the society pages and in the Texas magazines."

He shrugged. "I don't pay attention to those. They're meaningless. Ahh, here's our champagne."

Their waiter popped the cork, got Jake's approval of the champagne and then poured two flutes. As soon as they were alone, Jake raised his glass in a toast.

"Here's to a successful endeavor—with your help—of keeping my promises to Thane Warner." Looking into her brown eyes, Jake leaned forward to touch his flute lightly against hers. They each sipped and she swirled her drink slightly.

"After our brief look at the house today, I have a feeling this job may take several weeks. You and I have to go through all the stuff in the house, but once we do, I can get a crew to handle disposing of items, moving what you don't want to my store to sell. We can always have an auction for the rest, at a hotel or somewhere in Dallas. The ranch would not be a good place. It's going to be a big job, but I really don't want to charge you. I can so easily take my fee out of what Thane gave me."

He shook his head. "That was his gift to you for doing this, just as the Long L Ranch was his gift to me. Don't take the charges to me out of his gift. I feel honor bound to follow his wishes as much as I can and do what he intended."

She nodded. "Very well, I'll give you estimates on what it will cost you." She raised her flute to him. "Here's to the beginning of the end of the Ralston-Kincaid feud. May we work together in harmony and cooperation," she said, smiling at him.

He touched her flute with his. "As of now, that feud is over between us." They locked gazes and he couldn't look away as he sipped the bubbly champagne and ached to draw her into his arms.

"I ought to drink to working with you and keeping our relationship focused on business," she said, raising her flute again.

"I'll drink to that, too, because it keeps complications at bay and we may have enough of them just clearing out that house," he said, glad to hear that she wanted to keep everything between them strictly business. But it didn't stop or diminish one tiny fraction the reactions he was having to her. In spite of common sense, he was attracted to her.

"How did you get into this business?" he asked, trying to keep his focus where it belonged.

She shrugged. "I grew up around antiques so I know their value and their history. My art is my first love and I've been saving so I can let someone run the store for me and do the appraisals, then I'd be free to paint and draw full-time. I want my own gallery. Now, with Thane's check, I can do that and spend all my time painting and drawing. I'm thrilled by that prospect and can't wait to look for a place. There will be enough money for me to open a gallery where I can show and sell my paintings."

"Good. You said you're friends and work with Vivian Warner."

"Yes. She has galleries and she's a good artist."

As she talked to him, Emily's eyes sparkled and she sounded enthusiastic and her bubbly cheer made him want to reach out for her.

When he realized the drift of his thoughts, he changed the conversation. "I left a message for my contractor to go out and look at the house. I hope it's in good shape so I can keep it. It's entirely different from the house on my Hill Country ranch, the JR Ranch, which is one story and Western style."

"Today, I asked you if I could see your Dallas condo so I'd know what style of furniture you like. That really isn't necessary. Just send me a couple of pictures—and I'll know what you like."

Amused, he smiled. "Scared to go home with me?" he asked. Before she could answer, his smile vanished and he shook his head.

"See how easily I slip away from the business arrangement we have? Forget what I just asked. I was teasing you, anyway. I'll send the pictures."

"Good," she said, looking down at her drink,

but he saw her cheeks turn pink and he wondered whether she was thinking about their kiss today or that she had revealed she was still reacting to that kiss. Regardless, she was right—they were better off avoiding going to either home. Keep everything businesslike between them. How many times would he have to remind himself?

Their waiter appeared and placed a basket of hot wheat rolls on the table and took their dinner orders.

As soon as they were alone, Jake sipped the champagne. "Whenever you want to go to the ranch, tell me. We can fly because driving back and forth will eat up the time."

"The first thing is to get the cleaning done. I told you the cleaning is scheduled for Wednesday and the paint crews will start on the outside of the house on Wednesday. I'll see about buying furniture as soon as possible and get it delivered when the cleaning is over. The cleaning crews will stay at the motel in Flat Hill, so they'll be close and it won't take a lot of time to go back and forth. Three crews working long hours should get the job done quickly."

"That's excellent. I want to do this and get through with it."

Their dinners were served and as he ate his steak and she ate wild Alaskan salmon, they talked about the ranch house and kept the conversation centered on business, which she seemed just as happy to do as he was.

After dinner, when he turned up her drive and stopped near the house, she unbuckled her seat belt. "We're not on a date. It was a business meeting, so you don't have to walk me to the door. I can get in just fine and I have an alarm." She twisted in the seat to face him. "Thank you for dinner and I'm looking forward to this job."

"I'm glad you're willing to do it, although Thane's gift would convince nearly anyone to say yes. But I'm still walking you to the door." He got out before she could protest and as he went around the car, she stepped out.

They walked together to the porch and he crossed to the door to see that she got inside. She unlocked the door but didn't open it as she turned to Jake. "Again, thanks for hiring me, for this opportunity. I look forward to it. As for Thane Warner's gift—I'm still in a daze. It's the same as winning the lottery. Just amazing."

The porch light caused deep shadows, but soft light fell on her face, her prominent cheekbones, her full lips. His gaze lingered on her mouth and then he looked into her eyes that were filled with longing.

His pulse raced and he wanted to reach for her, to wrap his arms around her and put his mouth on hers and have one more earth-shattering kiss.

She was an employee. A Kincaid, he silently reminded himself. He repeated the litany to try to cool down, to back off when every inch of him wanted to reach for her.

He stepped back and smiled. "I'll call you," he said in a hoarse voice. He turned and left in long strides as if something was after him. Once behind the wheel in his car, he wiped his brow. He was hot, sweaty and he wanted her. He lowered the window and let the breeze blow on his heated body as he drove back to the street. But it did little to cool him off. They'd been together for one day and they had already had a first kiss—a stunning, unforgettable, life-changing first kiss. What was going to happen when they'd be living all alone out there on that ranch?

Four

On Friday, Emily was getting ready for an appointment at Jake's office at Ralston Investments, his family's investment firm, to give him an update on the situation at the ranch. She glanced at the pictures he had sent of his condo that took up the entire upper floor of a downtown office building he owned and she had to smile. The pictures didn't indicate his preference of style for the Long L Ranch because he had two entirely different styles—the condo had a kitchen and breakfast area that was sleek and contemporary with sparse lines and pale neutral colors. In contrast a great room had ornate French Louis XV fruitwood furniture. The furnishings were elegant with a spectacular crystal chandelier in the entryway and another in the dining room. So which did he want for the Long L? Or did he want another style entirely? When she sent him a text, he wrote back, Surprise me.

Annoyed at first, she had to laugh and shake her head. She suspected that was his way of saying he didn't want to be bothered. It was her choice to make, cost be damned.

She looked into her closet and dressed in comfortable jeans, a pale yellow sweatshirt and walking shoes. She braided her hair in one long braid behind her head and didn't wear makeup. She didn't know what stirred the fiery attraction between them—although she suspected that happened to him most of the time, but in this case, she was certain it was as unwanted by him as it was by her.

Jake had promised Thane he would do what he could to try to end the Ralston-Kincaid feud, but that was an impossible promise to keep. She couldn't keep from being aware all the time she was with a Ralston. His dad was a Ralston, his mother's first husband was a Ralston. She also reminded herself that he had a mixed-up family and she had nothing in common with Jake except that they were Texans. And they were both attracted to each other.

Last Friday night at her door, for an instant,

she had thought he was going to kiss her. Worse, she had wanted him to. What had happened to her common sense? Any attraction she yielded to with Jake Ralston would mean heartache ahead. Why was she attracted to him? That was a no-brainer. The man was to-die-for handsome. He was fun to be with, practical and coolheaded. Just look at the way he'd behaved with her brother. Jake had been calm, collected and amused by Lucas, who was seething with anger and ready for a fight.

In addition to handsome and levelheaded, Jake was sexy. Incredibly sexy. And she suspected he might be the best kisser this side of the Pacific and Atlantic Oceans.

Shaking her head, she realized she was lost in thought about him when she was due at his office soon. She grabbed her purse and slung it on her shoulder. Thirty minutes later, she walked into Jake's office and her heart skipped a beat.

In navy slacks, a white shirt and black boots, he came around his desk to greet her. A lock of his wavy black hair had fallen on his forehead. He flashed an inviting smile. "Have a seat," he said, motioning toward one of the leather chairs in front of his desk. His voice was a notch lower than normal. He stopped far enough away that she knew there would be no handshake between them. She sat in one of the brown leather chairs and noticed they were much farther apart than they had been in her office.

He sat in the other chair and faced her, stretching out his long legs and crossing them at the ankles. "What's the report?"

"I've bought the furniture and it's to be delivered tomorrow at about two. You said you didn't want to be consulted before I went ahead and bought the furniture. You can return it if you don't like it. I need to be out there, just for the day tomorrow when they deliver it. In fact, I'd like to get there early enough to check out the rooms."

"Good idea."

"By the way, the cleaning crew put aside papers they found for you to go through. I'll look at them if you'd like and try to weed out what I think you don't need to see."

"That would be excellent. Use your judgment because I don't give a damn about those old rascal grandfathers and their stuff."

"The cleaning crews will finish this morning, so when I get to your ranch, the place will be clean and ready for the furniture. Now, when I go tomorrow, I'm taking assistants with me. We can direct where the furniture will go as they unload it. I've already gone over it with them."

"Tell them they can fly out with us. And the cleaning was fast work."

"You paid extra," she said, smiling at him, and

he laughed with a flash of even white teeth that made him even more appealing.

"Why don't we fly to Flat Hill in the morning? Would you like to leave at seven o'clock?"

"That's perfect," she said. "I'll let the others know."

"Good. I'll pick you up."

"You don't need to taxi me around. I'll meet you at the airport. I know where you go now and I'll be there at seven o'clock."

He looked amused as he nodded. "Very well. I'll meet you there. I'm looking forward to seeing the house and getting started on clearing things out. I want to do this and be through with it and I know you do, too, especially since you can make the change to a full-time artist now."

"Oh, yes," she said, with more feeling than she should have—only because he'd smiled.

"We'll manage working out there together. Thanks for all you're doing," he said, standing as she did. "Just in case I forget to tell you tomorrow, good luck with your family Sunday evening when you break the news. I imagine your brother has already informed your family about our encounter."

"I'm sure he has and they'll all be curious, especially since I missed dinner this past Sunday. I'm ready for them."

"Just give me warning if I need to be on guard."

"Oh, no. My brothers won't get physical."

"I had a different impression with Lucas."

She smiled and shrugged. "Maybe. He probably knew I would stop him."

"Sure," Jake said and walked around the desk to go open the door for her. He kept space between them and held the door, stepping back. Even so, she felt a prickling awareness when she walked past him.

"See you in the morning."

"Thanks." She left, her back tingling because she suspected he was standing there watching her walk away, although she couldn't imagine why she would still interest him, especially in her old jeans and sweatshirt. She let out her breath. She had a smoldering awareness of him and all the time they had talked, she had tried to avoid looking at his mouth or thinking about his kiss, but that had been impossible. Next time with him should be easier because instead of a confined office, they'd be in a house big enough that they could avoid each other easily.

Now if only she believed that.

Glancing at his watch, Jake saw it was time for his lunch meeting with his ranger buddies. He made a few notes that were reminders for the afternoon and then left his office to drive to a popular lunch place near his office. It was a sunny September day in Dallas and he had reservations for a patio table.

In minutes, Mike Moretti appeared and Jake shook hands with him, his gaze running over

Mike's thick black hair. He wore a blue cotton long-sleeve Western shirt, jeans, with a big silver belt buckle he had won in a rodeo, and boots.

"You made the transformation from ranger to rancher well, I see."

"You bet. I'm living a good life out on the Tumbling T and I hope you feel the same about coming back."

"This beats getting ambushed any day," he said and they both smiled.

"Here comes Noah," Jake said, watching his friend walking toward them. Wind blew Noah's black curls and as he reached their table, his blue eyes sparkled and he had a big smile when he shook hands with his friends.

"It's good to see you guys. We thought you were never coming home," he told Jake.

"I was beginning to think that myself. But I'm here to stay now."

A waiter came with water and took drink orders, leaving them menus.

They talked about lunch, ordered shortly and then Jake turned to Mike. "You start and bring us up to date on what's going on."

"I feel as if I owe my world and my life to Thane. I couldn't be happier."

"That's good," Jake said. "You're obviously happily married and it's just as obvious you like being a rancher."

"Oh, yeah, but I always have been a cowboy, except for that military stint. We've got some really fine horses. The cattle are good. So far this fall we've gotten some rain so we're not in a terrible drought. It's good. Vivian and I are happy," he said. "It's a good life and I owe it to Thane."

"We all owe a lot to Thane," Noah added and they were quiet for a moment. "You'll have another ranch because of him," he said, looking at Jake, who nodded. "I have my family, Camilla and Ethan," Noah continued. "Ethan is such a joy. How about you?" he asked Jake. "How's the Long L? Have you looked at it?"

"Oh, yeah, and I'm glad to have it. The place needs a lot of work and there's no telling what we'll find."

"Thane had it up and going and it's a working ranch right now."

"How about the Ralston-Kincaid feud?" Noah asked.

"Emily agreed to work for me. She said that she had no choice when she saw the check Thane had given her." He looked at Mike. "If you were part of approving that check for her, thank you. She was about to turn me down on the job, but then I gave her that check and she didn't hesitate to accept when she saw it."

"Well, that was Vivian and Thane. I had nothing to do with that decision. I think Thane did all of what he wanted done, all the letters and gifts and promises. I think he was ready in case something happened to him. He wanted everything back home taken good care of with no loose ends."

Their reminiscences were halted when their cheeseburgers and onion rings were placed before them. When they were alone again, Jake told them about going to see Thane's folks. "It was hard to do, but I wanted to see them."

"I see them somewhat often because of marrying into the family. They've had a difficult time over their loss," Noah said. "Ethan is a joy to them and that helps."

"We invited them to our wedding, but they sent their regrets and I can understand," Mike said. "That would have been tough for them."

"So Emily Kincaid is going to work for you," Noah said. "Think Thane was trying to get you two together the way he did the four of us?"

Jake shook his head. "No, I think Thane saw it as a way of ending the Ralston-Kincaid feud. After more than a century, the feud is ridiculous. It's time it ended."

"I think Thane wanted it ended partly to help me in running the ranch," Mike said. "So far, I haven't had trouble from any of them, no Ralstons or Kincaids. The two of you working together should help end the feud. As long as people know about your business deal."

"Word gets around fast. I'll take her to dinner where we can be seen by Ralstons and Kincaids."

"Good luck with it," Noah said. "I hope you like that ranch."

"I hope you don't find any skeletons—real skeletons," Mike added. "The way Thane talked about those old grandfathers of his wasn't good. Vivian doesn't want to go near the place."

"She can't be as bad about that as Camilla," Noah added. "Camilla can barely stand cowboys or ranches because of her grandfather and that ranch. That almost kept us from marrying."

Jake was happy for his ranger buddies. They'd both found their callings and their true loves. But that last part wasn't something Jake wanted for himself.

After lunch, when he left to go back to the office, he was still thinking about the different lives he and his friends led now and how close they had been when in Afghanistan. He thought about Noah's question—had Thane hoped to get him together with Emily the way he had with Mike and Vivian, and Noah and Camilla? Jake really didn't think so. They were so different—no one could have predicted the heated reaction he and Emily had to any physical contact between them. There wasn't a reason for it and the sizzle should disappear when they started living together.

If Jake was wrong and that's what Thane had

hoped for, it wouldn't happen because he and Emily would never have a permanent relationship. She definitely wasn't his type and he definitely wasn't ready to marry, much less have a shred of interest in a woman who was totally tied into family.

But he did like to kiss her...

Ten minutes before 7:00 a.m. on Saturday morning, Emily parked and hurried to meet Jake where he waited by his private plane. He looked every inch the rancher this morning in his black hat. He had on a blue-and-black-plaid long-sleeve Western shirt, tight jeans and black boots, and the minute she saw him her heart jumped.

"Good morning," she said, smiling at him.

"For this early hour, you're filled with cheer. Where are your assistants?"

"They wanted to stay in Flat Hill last night and get an early start. Actually, I think they wanted to go out, have some fun and meet cowboys and cowgirls."

"Well, on most nights in Flat Hill, they can find some fun. So we'll meet them at the ranch. Let's board."

He took her arm, which surprised her because he hadn't come near her since their last kiss. He held her arm lightly and then let her go ahead of him on the steps into the plane. She had dressed for work in jeans, a blue T-shirt and sneakers. She had her hair in a braid and a blue ball cap.

When they stepped into the plane, he touched her arm and she turned to him.

"I'm your pilot and I have a very good, experienced copilot, so sit back and enjoy the ride," Jake said.

"I will," she said, smiling at him as she put her things in the overhead and sat to buckle her seat belt.

She watched Jake in the cockpit. His shoulders were broad and she remembered exactly how it felt to be held in his embrace, the solid muscles in his arms. He was a former US Army Ranger, strong and sexy. Maybe she should have left her brother alone and not interfered that night at the club. It would have served Lucas right if he'd tangled with Jake. But she was glad they hadn't fought because she wouldn't have wanted either one of them hurt.

Sunday night she would have to tell her family about her new job. They weren't going to like it. Could she convince them that what she was doing was a good thing for all of them?

It was Monday that she thought about the most—moving to the ranch with Jake and working with him constantly. Just the idea made her recall their fiery kiss. When they were under the same roof every night, how was she going to resist him? And would he even try to kiss her again? From the way he looked at her sometimes, she had a feeling he remembered their kiss as well as she did. And looked as if he wanted to repeat it.

She felt her pulse beat faster at the thought. She had to stop focusing on Jake's kiss, but she couldn't forget it or overlook it or even just stop thinking about it.

They taxied down the runway and soon were smoothly airborne, and she got out a notebook she carried to look at her schedule for the week. She couldn't wait to see the improvements on the house.

Sometime later when they drove up the road to the ranch, she saw them. The front first floor already had a fresh coat of white paint on the outside. Windows were clean, screens replaced. Fresh pots of palms were on the porch, and hanging baskets held various blooming flowers.

"The house looks good," he said. "Your crews are doing a bang-up job, and I heard back from my contractor just yesterday. He said the house is sound, so all this work won't be for nothing."

"That's great! And I think so, too." Four rocking chairs were on the porch and a porch swing had been hung, giving a charming appeal. "I'm glad you like it. I think it looks inviting and comfortable," she said.

Rum had been waiting and got out of his pickup to come meet them. As he shook hands with Jake and tipped his hat to Emily, he said, "The place is beginning to look mighty good."

"I'd like to go in and look at the house," Jake told him. "Come with us if you want, Rum."

"Thanks but I'll watch for the guys delivering furniture and try out one of the new rockers. These look first-rate. Nothing like a rocking chair."

Jake held a screen door for Emily and as she entered, she had that prickly awareness of passing so close to him. Too easily, she could recall their kiss and being pressed against him. Why couldn't she forget their kiss? She knew the answer and didn't want to think about it.

She tried to focus on the house that smelled of cleaning solutions and paint. "Oh, my, they have the fountain going." She looked at the splashing fountain and a pale aqua-and-gold marble pool. "Look at the marble. You couldn't see any colors when we were here before because of the dust. It's beautiful. And look at the hall," she said, turning.

The walls had fresh white paint, and the hall was now light and welcoming. The antique bench with new dark blue brocade upholstery that she'd had sent out from her Dallas shop would look beautiful here.

"I think this is all they have painted inside so far," she told him, "but you can see the interior is going to look inviting, too."

"Yes, it is. This floor is like new," Jake said,

indicating the wide oak planks that had been cleaned, polished and buffed.

"It looks like an entirely different place already."

"It does," he said and she looked up to see him staring at her. She felt a flutter dance up her spine and she forgot the house and the workers. For a moment, memories of his kiss consumed her and she felt hot with longing. She needed to move away from him, get away and leave him in a different room.

"We agree about the house. We agree about other things. We're each thinking about the same thing right now," he said in a husky voice that went over her like a caress.

"Jake, quit while you're ahead. Stick with business," she whispered, stepping back, her heart pounding because she felt he was about to reach for her and she wanted him to, but she knew better.

He blinked and turned away.

"You hired a good crew," he said after a moment.

"Thanks. They've concentrated on getting this first floor in shape because they knew we'd be staying here and the furniture's coming for these rooms. They'll get to the other floors this week. Even with three crews, it's going to take longer than we estimated."

"That's all right if it all turns out like this," he said and she wondered if he really would ever live on this ranch.

At 1:30 p.m. Jake received a call that the delivery trucks had left Flat Hill and soon would be at the ranch.

Emily went to the porch with Jake and Rum to wait and sooner than she expected, she saw a plume of dust stirred up on the road before three trucks came around a curve and into view.

Jake smiled. "I guess you bought me a lot of furniture."

"Yes, I did, as a matter of fact. Even a gym."

"Good deal. Comfy furniture and good food from the bunkhouse. We should get through this job fast."

"You go to your office and direct the delivery guys where to put the furniture. We'll take the other rooms."

"Works for me," he said.

The trucks parked and the man in charge met Emily and her assistants, and for the next two hours she was busy directing the men where to take the furniture. Her crew had new bedding washed and ready to put on the beds and by six, they had three furnished bedrooms, two offices, a partial gym, a new refrigerator and new microwave oven, as well as a table, chairs and some kitchen equipment. Some of the cowboys had come to help and when they stopped working, Jake thanked each one and Rum.

Finally, her assistants left to drive back to their hotel; since Jake and Emily were returning Monday, they'd be staying in Flat Hill for the next few weeks, as well. Emily left with Jake to fly home and he insisted on taking her to dinner, something casual where they wouldn't have to change.

It was ten o'clock that night when he finally drove her home. When he stopped on the driveway, she turned to him. "I said it before—this isn't a date and you don't have to walk me to the door."

"It isn't exactly a chore," he said, stepping out and coming around the car to walk with her. "I want to thank you for all you've done already. Today went well. I didn't think we could get all that done so quickly."

"We've moved people before so you get used to doing it," she said, but she was thinking about Jake walking close beside her. They had been busy throughout the day, but in the plane and through dinner, she'd become increasingly aware of him. There was no way to stop the physical reaction she had to him except to keep busy every second or stay away from him. Could she stick to business when they were at the ranch?

She hoped so, but at this point, the answer didn't matter. She had made the commitment and she was leaving to work on the ranch with Jake the day after tomorrow. Surely, she could control her actions and her responses and keep from falling in love with him.

Her answer had to be yes, but she worried about it. She had never been drawn to a man the way she was to Jake and she didn't understand his appeal. He wasn't her type. He didn't want a relationship any more than she did. He didn't flirt and there were times he was careful to avoid contact. In spite of that, she had a tingly awareness of him any time she was near him and right now was no exception.

Her pulse was racing when they got to the door. She needed to say good-night, step inside and close the door. No kissing. No touching.

"Thank you for dinner, Jake," she said without looking at him. "I'll meet you at the airport Monday morning—" Her speech halted when his hand closed lightly on her upper arm and he gently turned her to face him.

"Are you scared of me?" he whispered and stepped closer.

"I'm scared of me," she answered.

"Another kiss isn't going to change your life or mine. Lighten up a little. It's just a kiss," he whispered and all the time he talked, he leaned closer and drew her to him. He tightened his arm around her waist and placed his mouth on hers and her argument ended.

Her knees almost buckled and heat filled her while her heart raced. His mouth was on hers, his tongue over hers, his arm holding her tightly against his solid body. Common sense whispered to stop kissing him. Instead, she slipped her arm around his neck, pressed against him and opened her mouth to him, to kiss him as if it might be her last.

He wrapped both arms around her and pulled her even more tightly against him, making her want nothing more than to go inside her house, shut the door and kiss the night away. Never had kisses been like this. She couldn't stop, not yet. She ran her fingers in his hair above his nape, and then let her hand slide down across his broad shoulder.

His hand ran over her bottom, stroking her lightly and pulling her against him even more, if that was possible. His touch set her on fire, threatening to singe her heart, and she shifted, trying to grasp a lifeline for reason and resolve.

When she pushed slightly, he released her.

She stepped back and they both gasped for breath as they looked at each other, and she fought the temptation to walk back into his arms—or to draw him into the house and into her bed.

She clung to common sense enough to resist. She stepped inside her doorway. "Lighten up a little, you said. That kiss could have destroyed every lick of common sense and caution I have. Jake, we've got to work together."

"I promise you that our kisses won't interfere with our working together. Not at all."

"Maybe you can take them more casually than I can."

"If I had even the tiniest degree more of a reaction to them, I would burst into flames."

"Then I know just what I need to do." She opened the door wider and turned back to him.

"Good night, Jake. I'll see you Monday morning at the airport." She closed the door and leaned against it, gasping for air, her heart pounding. She had just made another big mistake by kissing him again. Why couldn't she resist him? She knew the answer to that question. Because she'd never been kissed the way Jake kissed her.

But this was a business deal. A business deal with a man whose kisses dazzled her more than that million-dollar check from Thane Warner.

She didn't realize how long she had been standing there just thinking about Jake long after she heard him drive away. In spite of all the work today, she knew sleep would be impossible. Tomorrow she would be away from Jake and, hopefully, she'd cool down.

Tomorrow night she would also be with all her family and she would tell them that she was employed by Jake Ralston. That would be the first time ever she knew of a Ralston and a Kincaid working together.

There was one little glimmer of something positive she could take from this situation. Jake's kisses had ended any Ralston-Kincaid feud between them. That had vanished, along with her common sense and willpower.

Five

By Sunday, she was ready to deal with her family and to break the news to them about Jake Ralston and Thane's gift to her. She was dressed in a navy suit and a navy silk blouse, with her hair in a bun on the back of her head. She wanted to look businesslike, collected and in charge when she faced her family. Her sister, Andrea, was married and had a fifteen-month-old baby girl and a little boy who was three. On Sunday nights, their paternal grandparents joined the Kincaids for dinner, so once everyone arrived, there were sixteen of them who'd hear her news.

She heard the scrape of boot heels on the wood

floor and Lucas stepped into the hall of her parents' home. He stopped in front of her. "You're dressed up for Sunday night. Are we going to hear why you were with Jake Ralston?"

"Yes. I told you to just wait until I could talk to all the family at once."

"Good," he said, turning to walk with her to the great room where the family always gathered. "I can't imagine any reason to associate with a low-life Ralston."

"Lucas, Jake Ralston is a former US Army Ranger. He is not a 'low-life' and I don't want to hear that about him again."

Lucas's eyes narrowed. "Are you in love with him?"

"Absolutely not. I told you, this is business. Pay attention. Are you ready to join the family?"

"Yes. I'm not going to miss hearing why you were with a Ralston."

"Whatever reason I was with him, I did not appreciate you trying to start a fight in the lobby. Mom wouldn't be overjoyed with that one, either."

"Well, maybe not. He's not coming to our house, is he?"

"You're acting like a little kid. Can't you wait so I don't have to say everything twice?"

"I'll wait. This better be good."

"It is, Lucas. It's very good."

As they entered the great room, Simon, her

three-year-old nephew came running to hug her. She picked him up to hug him and then he turned, holding his arms out to Lucas, who took him and swung him overhead, making him giggle.

Emily saw her little fifteen-month-old niece, Sheila, holding on to furniture and trying to come greet her. Emily picked up Sheila and hugged her, smiling at her. "Don't you look pretty with pink hair bows and your pink jumper."

Next, she greeted her parents and grandparents, then went into the kitchen to say hello to the cook and her daughter. It was her regular Sunday-night ritual. The aroma of Sunday-night favorites, Texas chili and hot corn bread, filled the kitchen.

She'd just stepped back into the great room when her brother Doug and his wife, Lydia, appeared. Her brother headed straight toward Emily.

"I hear you were in town with Jake Ralston," Doug said.

"And did Lucas tell you it was business and that I intend to talk to all of you about it tonight?" she asked, smiling at her oldest brother. Doug had the same blond hair as the rest of the family, and his eyes were a dark blue.

"I hope you had a good reason to be with a Ralston."

"You and Lucas can tell me in a little while if I did."

Over the next hour, she enjoyed her dinner, sitting between her sister and her little niece. Emily loved the Sunday-evening ritual. She thought about Jake and what he missed by not having family like she did.

She waited until Violet and her daughter had finished with the kitchen, closed for the night and went home so only the family was present. Simon slept in his dad's arms, and Sheila sat on her grandmother's lap and played with her doll. Emily got her small carrying case and asked for everyone's attention.

"I have some news for all of you. You all know that Thane Warner lost his life in Afghanistan. Thane was fatally wounded in an ambush and as he was dying, he asked his three close friends to promise to do something for him when they returned home. Mike Moretti, who you remember married Thane's widow, Noah Grant, who married Thane's sister, and the third one was Jake Ralston. He asked Jake Ralston to hire me to help him clear all the belongings at his grandfather's Long L Ranch and restore the house. Thane inherited his grandfather's ranch."

"That old reprobate was a crook," her dad said, shaking his head. "I'm talking about Clem Warner, Thane's grandfather. You're not going to work for Jake Ralston, are you?" her dad asked.

"Yes, I am. Please listen, because this was done in the last few minutes of Thane Warner's life. I think everyone in our family likes the Warners and liked Thane. He gave his life for his country. Now, the least you can do is listen to what he wanted and why."

"We're listening," Doug said. "And everyone here did like Thane."

"For following Thane's wishes, he deeded the Long L to Jake Ralston, and for me doing the job, Thane sent along a gift. It has nothing to do with my payment from Jake for doing the work I'll do. I made a copy of my gift from Thane and will pass it around so all of you can see. Lucas, you can start and tell everyone what I received. Before you do, let me tell you that Vivian, Thane's wife, knew about this gift and approved of it."

Emily handed a paper to her brother who looked at it and looked at her with wide eyes. Then he turned to the family. "Thane gave her a check for a million dollars."

Everyone started talking at once, except for Lucas and Doug who both turned to her. "If Thane Warner gave that to you, then it is legitimate. Thane was as honest as they come," Lucas said.

"You're a millionaire now," Doug said, looking intently at her. "You can hire someone to run the shop and paint, which is what you wanted to do."

"I guess I did interfere the other night," Lucas said. "I thought you were on a date."

"I know you did." She smiled at him and waited

a moment while her family talked. She saw her dad looking at her and she gave him a smile.

"You've decided what you're going to do, haven't you?" he asked her.

"Yes, I have." She raised her voice and everyone became quiet. "Thane wanted three things—for Jake to hire me and for us to do the job together. As for the third... First, let me say that I plan to keep only half of this check. The other half I will divide evenly with all of you in this room, including the children."

Everyone started talking again and she waved her hand. "Let me finish. Thane asked Jake to promise to do what he could to end the Ralston-Kincaid feud. Well, it's impossible for Jake to end a feud that's over a hundred and fifty years old, but he can do some things to start and so can I. If you accept this money, I want you to try to do your part to end this feud. Don't take the money if you're going to continue not speaking to Ralstons and doing things to promote the feud. We have to start somewhere. There are two little children in this room who'll never hate a Ralston if they are not taught to hate them." She saw her dad smile at her and give her a thumbs-up, which told her she had his support.

"Now, I have a check for each of you, which I'll hand out. If you don't want to end this feud, then don't take the check. And that includes being co-operative and friendly with Jake Ralston."

She held out an envelope to Doug and he took it. "I'll still compete with Jake if he signs up for a rodeo," he said.

"That doesn't matter and isn't part of the feud."

He shrugged and tapped the envelope. "You're sure you want to do this? You're giving away money you could use."

"I'm sure. It's to my family. That's different. And I don't want a hassle, either, about working for Jake," she said, looking at Lucas.

"I got the message and I won't hassle him," Doug agreed.

"That's good to hear."

"I'm like Doug," Lucas said when she turned to him. "Are you sure you want to give away half of your money?"

"I'll still have a lot of money and if this helps end that old feud, then that was what Thane wanted."

She had to reassure each family member in turn but finally she was finished. When she turned, Lucas appeared at her side. He put his hands on his hips. "We may bring a little peace to the Ralston-Kincaid feud, but don't go out there and fall in love with Jake Ralston, because he isn't a mar-rying man."

She had to laugh. "Lucas, thank you for the advice. I'll remember that when I'm working with Jake."

"You're laughing at me. Be careful, Emily. That guy draws in women like a rock star and he isn't going to settle down. His family is so mixed up— his mother has married two Ralstons and I know that Jake and his dad aren't close at all. That isn't the kind of family you have."

Her smile faded. "I know that, Lucas. He's not my type, anyway, and I'm not his, and we both know it." That didn't stop her from remembering Jake's kisses, though. "I can take care of myself and I don't attract men like Jake."

"Oh, yes, you will. Just be careful. Listen, are you staying out on that ranch with him?"

"Yes. It's a working ranch, so there are a bunch of people and they have a security crew and a guy named Rum in charge of the house. He's nice and he hangs out sometimes at the house. Remember, Thane wanted Jake and me to work out there together. He wouldn't try to set me up to work with Jake if he didn't trust Jake completely."

"You have a point there. And he wouldn't have trusted him to deliver a cashier's check for a million dollars, either, so I guess Jake is an okay guy."

"He's more than an okay guy because he risked his life for his country."

"I'm glad about that guy, Rum, hanging out around the house and having a security crew, but you're right. Thane wouldn't ever put you in jeopardy and he should know Jake as well as himself. Those two had a lifelong friendship. If you want me, though, for any reason, text and I'll be there."

"Thank you, big brother," she said, smiling at him.

"You guard your heart," he repeated. "That's where Jake's a threat. I've been to parties and gone out with his old girlfriends and they don't get over him. Just be careful."

"Lucas, you should have quit when you were ahead. Now, I'm cutting this short. I have to go home to get ready for tomorrow. That house is going to be a lot of work and we're trying to do it fast to get through it."

"That's also good to hear." His smile faded. "Thanks for sharing your good fortune with the family. That's generous and I think everyone will think twice about the old feud. Thane was right. The money will be a big reminder. And you're right about the kids. Simon and Sheila shouldn't be taught to hate. Thane would be pleased."

"I hope our family can help. You have to start somewhere. This feud is ridiculous when you think about it."

"Listen, this is generous and so very nice, but you know my business is growing. Take my check back. I appreciate this, but I don't need it and I know you can put it to use somewhere."

"Thanks, Lucas," she said, smiling at him. "That's really sweet, but you keep it. You'll figure out something to do with it that will do some good. I already have enough to be able to paint full-time when I'm through with this job for Jake. I'll be finding someone to run my shop. I'm fine."

"Hey, that's good news. Let me know when you do."

"I will. Now it's time for me to go. I've got a busy month ahead of me." They walked back to the great room together and she moved around the room, hugging and kissing her family and telling them goodbye. Minutes later, she was in her car and saw a text from Jake.

He insisted on picking her up Monday morning so she could leave her car at home. They agreed on 6:30 a.m. and she spent the next couple of hours packing and getting things ready to go. She had two women who would run the store while she was gone, so she didn't have to worry about that. In addition, her assistants, who had remained in Flat Hill this weekend, would meet them at the ranch.

Emily thought about how soon she would be under the same roof with Jake. Could she handle that or was she just going to melt into his arms and lose all good sense because of his fabulous kisses? She didn't want to end this job brokenhearted and in love with a man who wasn't interested in marriage, and wasn't like the men in her family. Yet, there was no way to forget his kisses. And there was no stopping the longing to kiss him again. So far, all he had to do was look at her and all her resolve melted. Could she work closely with him for the next few weeks and keep her heart locked away? And say no to the greatest kisses ever?

Lucas

Lucas saw his sister leave and walked to the front window to watch her drive away. While he stood there, Doug stopped beside him.

"I still don't like Jake."

"If we take the money, we'll have to be nicer to him," Lucas said.

"My conscience would hurt otherwise because she gave up half a mill to get her family's cooperation. We owe it to Em because she didn't have to share a penny of that money with us. And we owe it to Thane who was a great guy. I'll try to ignore Jake," Doug said. "We have to be nice to the Ralstons now."

"That's right," Lucas replied. "If we take the money, we're nice to the Ralstons—including Jake. She did point out that Thane set up her working on the ranch for and with Jake. Thane trusted Jake or he would never have done that."

Doug nodded. "She's right. Thane fought with

this guy in Afghanistan, so he knew he could trust him."

"Aw, hell, they'd been friends since they were in kindergarten or earlier. Thane had to know Jake through and through. Thane was sharp. He wouldn't have put her in jeopardy. Who would you trust to give a cashier's check for a million and ask him to deliver it to someone else? No one else in the world would have known except Vivian, who probably wouldn't have checked to see whether or not Jake delivered it."

"Thane usually knew what he was doing, so I hope he did on this. Even so, I'll be glad when she's through working with Jake."

"I'm going to invest my money, let it earn interest and somewhere down the line, give the original amount back to her," Lucas said.

"I'll go in with you. I think that's a good idea because I don't want to take her money, either. I'll feel better giving it back to Emily." Doug turned away from the window. "I'm leaving."

Lucas nodded and strolled behind his brother to tell the family goodbye. He left, driving back to the condo he had on the top floor of a fourteen-story office building he owned in a suburban area of Dallas. He would fly back to his ranch in his private plane tomorrow. His family—all of them except the little kids—were steeped in dislike for any Ralston—how could they suddenly turn around and change? He didn't think they could. On the other hand, Thane wouldn't have pushed for it if he hadn't thought it was possible.

Lucas could think of one Ralston he would be happy to speak to and to get to know better, and now maybe he had an excuse. Harper Ralston designed and sold her own jewelry in a small shop in the building next door. They never spoke, but he was certain she was as aware of him as he was of her. Thane had tossed in a million to Emily, plus a ranch to Jake, to try to get cooperation on ending the feud, so to please his sister Lucas would speak to Harper Ralston. It would be okay. His sister was working for a Ralston now and the sun still came up in the mornings.

Lucas smiled and whistled as he drove home. He would drop by the jewelry store before he went home to the ranch and see if he could have a conversation with a Ralston.

Monday morning, Jake picked up Emily promptly at 6:30 a.m. Her heartbeat quickened as she watched his long stride when he headed toward her front door.

She swung open the door and smiled, her pulse taking another jump when she looked into his dark brown eyes. "I'm ready to go. I have some things here I want to take with me."

"I'll get them," he said, shouldering a big bag and picking up two more.

He might not notice her in sweats and jeans, but there was no way she could keep from noticing him. Every second she was near him, she was conscious of him. There was no way to turn off that tingling awareness of him. It was as unwanted as it was unstoppable.

Her brothers' warnings echoed in her ears. Especially the reminder that Jake wouldn't settle down and didn't want a family and if she got involved with him, she would get hurt. She knew Lucas was absolutely convinced of that. She had to agree because there was good reason to think loving Jake would be disastrous. He had a stream of broken hearts in his wake, women who still loved him while Jake moved on and didn't look back. She reminded herself it was just a job. All she was doing was working for him. Employer and employee. She would be busy with the contents of the house while he would be busy with other things. *Stop worrying about being in the same house*, she reminded herself.

Through the flight to Flat Hill and then the drive in a limo to the ranch, Jake was professional, engrossed in papers he had brought, while she went over notes and looked at pictures of various furnishings in the house.

When they drove up to the house, painters were at work, trucks lined the drive and gardeners were digging new beds for flowers. There were men putting up wrought-iron fence sections to enclose a yard around the house.

Emily had done what she wanted with the house because Jake had insisted care and price didn't matter.

"You'll be getting bills for furniture, both indoor and outdoor, as well as all the other things that were necessary to get us set up here," she told him as they came to a stop. "I've hired a decorator for later and I'll work with her."

"That's fine. When this ranch is in shape, I'll probably live at my JR Ranch in the Hill Country and continue to let the man Thane hired run this ranch. When I'm not here, I'll just have a skeleton crew take care of the house."

"It's a lot of expense for an empty house."

He shook his head. "The ranch will pay for it. This is a very good ranch, with good men hired by Thane and water and mineral rights."

Jake held the door for her and brought her things inside.

Their job was about to begin in earnest.

Jake spent the morning and into the afternoon going through old legal documents, newspapers, letters, receipts, some papers dating back to the late 1800s. He sat at his new desk with a table beside him that was covered in papers, also near him was a trash barrel piled high with letters and newspapers. Close at hand was an open trunk filled with more papers.

He found several letters with sweeping penmanship by Thane's great-grandmother and more letters written by one of Thane's great-grandfathers.

Jake looked up when Emily knocked and entered.

"You're frowning. Are you having difficulties in here?" she asked as she sat in a chair facing him.

Momentarily he forgot the letter as his gaze swept over her. She wore her usual plain garb of loose-fitting jeans and a sweatshirt. She shouldn't have made his pulse jump and made him forget what he was doing, but she did. She made him forget everything except the kisses they'd shared. Her tempting mouth was rosy and as he looked at her full lips, he remembered kissing her. Sizzling kisses that shook him to the core. How could Emily, his employee, of all the women on earth, be the sexiest kisser in his life? He didn't want that discovery. He didn't want it at all, but every time he saw her, he wanted to kiss her again. She had muddled his life and caused problems he had never before encountered.

He remembered the letter he held and handed it to her. "I found a letter by Thane's great-grandfather. It was in answer to a man he owed money to and his great-grandfather wouldn't pay it back. The man threatened to kill him. That didn't happen, but it makes me wonder what Thane's great-grandfather did. Reading the letter, I got the feeling it was not an idle threat."

"'Either I get my money back or one of us dies,'" she read aloud.

"It wasn't Thane's great-grandfather who died. At least, that's not how he died. I've heard Thane tell that his great-great-grandfather killed a guy in a duel."

"Thane's family is quite nice and he turned out all right. Toss the letter and forget it."

"Probably a good idea." Jake looked at her intently and stood to walk around the desk to place his hands on the arms of her chair and lean close. He caught a scent of flowers as he looked into her big brown eyes. Her lips had parted and he heard her take a deep breath. "There are moments when I want to toss this employer-employee relationship right out the window and be just a man and a woman who are friends," he said in a husky voice.

"We can be friends," she whispered, shaking her head, "but we need to hang on to that employer-employee relationship. I don't want to end this job with a broken heart."

"A few fun kisses won't break your heart and you're too smart to fall in love with me," he said in a husky voice as he tightened his grip on the chair arms to keep from wrapping his arms around her and pulling her up against him. He placed one hand on her throat. "Your pulse is pounding as fast as mine. I think you want to kiss as much as I do."

"Maybe so, but I'm not going to complicate my life and every kiss makes me want to kiss you even more than I did so you back off."

"That's not the way to tell me to back off. Ahh, Emily—"

"Move away, Jake, and get a grip on common sense."

"Common sense isn't what I want to grab."

"You do it, anyway," she said.

He knew she was right. "Whatever the lady wants—" He stepped away.

"You go back behind your desk and I'll go back to what I was doing."

Nodding, he turned to walk to the other side of his desk. "There are just moments when I forget the employer-employee relationship we have."

"Read the old letters and maybe you'll forget all about everything else."

"Emily, I will never forget our kisses as long as I live," he said quietly and she blinked.

"That information isn't helping."

"Maybe one big kiss would satisfy me and I could settle back to work."

Smiling, she shook her head. "Nice try. No."

He grinned and was glad she was making light of the moment. She was right and he should keep that employer-employee status, but after the few hot kisses between them, there was no way he could resist trying to kiss her again. He wanted her naked, in his arms, in his bed, and that wouldn't happen without a lot of kisses.

She looked at the trash bin he had and lifted a letter out of it. "Have you read all these? This one doesn't look as if anyone has touched it."

"No. I'm just picking some at random. There's too much stuff here to go through all of it. So far it's trash."

She looked at the letters spread before him, the bin of letters and the box on the other side of his desk. She looked back at him.

"If you don't approve, you can say so. You think I should read each and every one. That's a lot of old letters and maybe it's best to let them go without anyone today knowing what's in there."

"You might miss something, like discovering Thane's family owns another ranch in Texas."

"It's true. You never know. Thane's family has one deep love that has run through generations— land. That's why they have so many ranchers in his family." He sighed. "Okay, I'll read a few more and then go find you and you can do what you want with them."

"Fair enough. Let me know when to start reading," she said sweetly and left the room.

He thought about a dinner he had been invited to attend as an honoree for a charity when he helped to rescue dogs from a disaster area. He hadn't thought about whom he would invite to go with him to the formal dinner and dance. But now he knew he wanted to ask Emily. That would be crossing the line again with an employee, but he wanted to dance with her and hold her in his arms. He wanted to touch and kiss her. And most of all, he wanted to seduce her.

If he did, he'd be asking for a boatload of trouble. Common sense said to keep his distance and not to invite her to a dinner dance. She was his employee. Stick to business—that's what he needed to do.

To that end, he spent another hour going through more old papers and pictures of people he didn't recognize. There still was the trunk full of papers. He was tired of the old documents and took up an armload to dump into the bin for Emily to read. He reached for another armload and saw a black box taped to the inside of the trunk. Curious, he pulled it out and opened it to find one letter inside in a pink envelope addressed to Ben Warner, Thane's dad. It was obviously from a woman and he wondered if Ben had put it in the box and hidden it near the bottom of the trunk. He guessed it might have been a love letter written to Ben from Celeste Warner, Thane's mother, but then he recognized the return address. Suddenly he sat up and stared at the pink envelope. He frowned because the return address was where his grand-mother lived. He looked at the flowing letters in cursive that spelled out *Ben Warner*. Startled, he recognized his mother's handwriting.

Curious about a letter that had been from his mother to Ben Warner, Jake pulled folded pink papers out to read and a faded photograph dropped into his hand. He was riveted by another shock because he recognized his own baby picture with his mother holding him. His mother had one just like it framed on her vanity. Stunned, he looked again at the envelope and saw it was sent about a month after he was born.

He looked at familiar handwriting. "My darling Ben: I should not write you, but I know you are home alone now while Celeste takes your baby son to see his grandparents. I won't write again, but I want you to have a picture of our baby."

"I'll be damned," Jake said aloud without realizing it. Stunned he stared at her words and looked again at his faded baby picture. Ben Warner was his real father. Thane Warner was his half brother. Jake held the letter up to continue reading:

"Since we live so close, with only two houses between your home and mine, I know you will see your son eventually. He is a fine baby. I know, too, we have done the right thing, but you have my heart. I will always love you. We are close enough so you can see our son grow up and I know the baby boy that you and Celeste have is a joy. Hopefully, our boys will be friends and you will see him often. I will always be close to you. I will always love you. We're neighbors and it is a comfort to me to know you are close. Dwight knows this is not his son. He does not know the father's identity. Only you and me and my doctor. Destroy this letter. I love you always."

Stunned, Jake stared out the window without seeing anything except an image of Ben Warner smiling at him and then drawing him close for a hug and telling him how glad he was that he'd made it home.

"I'll be damned," Jake said aloud. He and Thane were half brothers. It amazed him. And maybe it explained why they got along so well together. And why Thane's dad had always had such an interest in him. Now he knew why Ben Warner was so happy to see him. Why he felt closer to Ben Warner than he did to Dwight Ralston, the man he had always thought was his father.

"Thane, you should have read the letters," Jake whispered, wondering what Thane would have felt and knowing his answer as quickly as the question came. Thane would have been delighted to find out they were half brothers.

Jake thought about his mother, who had carried that secret all these years.

Jake looked up as he spoke. "Thane, my buddy,

how I miss you now. I wish you were here. We'd get a beer and sit down and discuss this discovery that we're half brothers. My life just changed forever." Jake rubbed the back of his neck and thought about Thane. "Ah, damn, I wish you were here."

"Your wish is granted, my friend. Here I am," came a lilting voice filled with laughter and Emily appeared again. She looked around. "And you are talking to—"

"Sit down, Emily," he said, coming to his feet when she entered the room. He pulled the straight chair around. "You take my captain's chair. It's more comfy than this one. I'll get us a drink. What do you want? Wine or beer?"

She laughed again and sat in the straight chair. "Do you think it's happy hour? I'll have a glass of water."

"Not this time. I think you'll want to join me. We're through working for a few hours at least. It is already four o'clock."

"Now I am curious. You're talking to yourself and you want a drink. And you want to discuss something with me, and I'm sure it's not the weather from the way you're acting."

"It's a very deep secret that this old house has divulged to me, and I will to you, and then we'll talk about it."

"Oh, goodie," she said and smiled, taking his mind off his discovery because her smile made him want to hold her in his arms again. "I think you found a family secret. Or maybe a gold mine somewhere on the ranch. Is that it?"

"You were closer when you were talking about a family secret. And it's better than a gold mine."

"Well, Thane said his grandfathers were rascals, so I'm surprised this is a family secret that is better than a gold mine."

"You will be surprised. I wish Thane were here so I could share it with him. But in his place I think you may be the perfect person. First, let's have a drink and for just a moment, I want to celebrate my discovery."

"Ah, at least it's good news."

"I think it's super great news. I just wish I had discovered it a lot sooner. White or red wine, or beer?" he asked again.

"Red wine, please. Now I'm very curious."

Jake opened a bottle and poured a glass of wine, crossing the room to hand it to her. His hand brushed hers and he felt that sizzle again. He tried to bank desire and memories that made him want to forget everything else and kiss her, but when he looked down into her eyes, he was struck by a thought.

He was surprised he hadn't realized it sooner. But now he did and the impact wasn't lost on him.

There was no longer the division between him and Emily. No longer a feud.

Because she was a Kincaid...and he wasn't a Ralston.

But she still wasn't his type of woman. He was doing what he knew he shouldn't and had said he wouldn't—getting to know her, kissing her when he had the opportunity. He had known better than to kiss her. Emily would never take sex in a casual way and he didn't want it any other way. In spite of knowing that, he couldn't resist her.

His brothers, parents and stepparents had soured him on marriage. Emily looked the type to equate sex with marriage and she also looked the type to not care how old-fashioned that was.

So why was his pulse still racing, and why did he still want to pull her into his arms and kiss her and carry her to his bed?

He went back to open a bottle of cold beer and took a swallow, then he pulled a chair close to hers. "My secret is just for the two of us for now. Thane threw us together here in this old house and I'm beginning to wonder why. To what extent he wanted us to try to end this Ralston-Kincaid feud."

"I think we're doing what he wanted."

Jake handed her the letter. "Read this and you'll discover the secret the same way I did."

Six

Emily took the letter, her warm fingers brushing his, and began to read while he waited.

"Oh, my word." She looked up and her eyes were wide. "You and Thane were half brothers," she said, sounding as stunned as he felt.

"And I never knew it until I read that letter."

"Oh, my heavens. Ben Warner is your father. No one knows this?"

"No one knows except my mom, Thane's dad, a doctor somewhere, and now you and I know."

"Wow. You're not a Ralston."

Jake smiled as he nodded. "That's right and suddenly people who have hated me will like me."

"That makes the feud even sillier."

"Maybe so, but we won't be the shining example now of how a Ralston and a Kincaid can get along," he replied.

"We can be if we don't tell anyone about your discovery. No one has to know. Thane is gone. It won't change your life. You don't want to hurt Ben Warner. You don't want to hurt your mother or Mrs. Warner. None of them will know if you keep it a secret—at least for a while longer. Mr. Warner has lived with it all these years. So has your mother. You might think twice before you reveal it to anyone else."

"I agree. I guess that's why Mr. Warner was always so interested in me and how I was getting along. I wish Thane had known, but we were like brothers, anyway. Maybe that's why the man I thought was my dad wasn't interested in me. I just thought he was cold."

"What about your birth certificate?"

"It says Dwight was my dad, but my guess is that a big sum of money exchanged hands to get that birth certificate and the doctor signed off on it."

Jake tilted his head to look intently at her. "I don't want to hurt Mom and I don't want to hurt the Warners. I think I should destroy the letter and keep it a secret."

While she sat thinking about it, he did, too.

"I think you should keep the secret," she said

finally. "It should be up to your mom if she ever wants to tell. Besides, you may do more good about ending the feud if you don't tell."

"True... I'm not going to tell anyone, except you, for a while. Once it's said, it can't be taken back."

"That's true and it could hurt Thane's mother."

"I never want to do that. I might just shred the letter."

"Well, you might want to think about that one. The letter is the only proof you have."

"We can always have a DNA test. I'll put the letter in the safe and keep it for now." He shook his head as a thought came to him. "I'm glad I never wanted to date Camilla Warner."

"I'm surprised you didn't, except she's—as you would say—not your type."

He shrugged. "She was always around and she seemed young. There just were no sparks at all and I never thought about taking her out," he said. The moment he mentioned sparks, he thought about the sparks flying each time he was near Emily.

He looked into her big brown eyes and knew that's what she was thinking also. A blush made her cheeks pink.

He forgot his heritage and its surprising revelation so many years later and thought about kissing Emily. As he looked into her eyes again, he guessed she was thinking the same as he was. With deliberation, he set aside the papers and his beer and stood, crossing the small space to her chair.

"Jake," she whispered.

He put his hands on the arms of her chair again and looked at her as he leaned close in front of her. "The look in your eyes gives you away. One kiss can't hurt," he said softly, his pulse drumming while he had an inner fight between what he wanted and what he knew he should do.

"One kiss can change history," she whispered.

"Oh, no, we won't let that happen," he said, placing his hands on her waist and pulling her to her feet and into his arms.

"Jake, this is so wrong."

"I don't think one tiny thing is wrong with it. We're single. We're adults," he whispered, brushing her ear with his lips. She was soft, sweet-smelling and her luscious curves were pressed against him as he placed his mouth on hers. Her softness set him on fire while his tongue claimed possession and his arm tightened around her. Holding her, he kissed her and felt her heart pounding against his chest. He wanted to get rid of the barrier of clothes between them. He wanted to kiss, to touch and to discover every inch of her and to make love to her for an entire night.

Kissing him in return, she wrapped her arms around his neck and pressed against him. His temperature climbed and he shook with wanting her.

She could tie him in knots with need the way no other woman ever could.

Hc shifted slightly, his hand caressing her throat, slipping down over her soft breast, which made his heart pound. He slipped his hands beneath her tan sweatshirt and cupped her breast over a flimsy lace bra. He pushed her shirt higher, released her bra and filled his hands with her breasts. His thumbs played lightly over her nipples.

Moaning softly, she clung to his upper arms. "Jake," she whispered. "Jake, slow down." She wiggled away from him while she gasped for breath and pulled her bra and sweatshirt back in place.

She was gorgeous and the meager taste of her that he'd had made his heart pound loud in his ears. He had never wanted a woman as badly as he did Emily at that moment. Employer and employee didn't matter and he didn't think it mattered at the moment to her, either. Desire was mutual. Even though she had ended the kiss, she wasn't walking away. Instead, she was breathing fast and staring at him as if he were the last man on earth and they had only an hour to live.

"We're in a business arrangement and we shouldn't kiss," she whispered.

"It's too late for that and this business arrangement is temporary, trivial in the overall picture. I think we can forget that excuse because we've already crossed that line and turned around and erased it."

"You're not helping."

"Well, there's a reason. You know what I want? I just want to—"

"Stop," she said, shaking her head at him. "I don't want to hear what you want. We need to use some sense and caution here so we can get this job done."

"We'll get it done in good order, okay? If you want, we'll back off anything personal now," he said even though that was the last thing he wanted to do.

"I think that's a good idea."

He placed his fingers lightly on her throat, feeling her racing pulse. "So why is your heartbeat racing?"

"You know what you do to me, what we do to each other. But that doesn't make it a good idea to continue."

"Oh, darlin', what we do to each other is rare and marvelous and I don't want to stop and you don't want to stop, either."

"I will, though. We just started restoring this old house. I'm not going to fall into your arms and into your bed the first night we're together out here. That can't happen," she said, trying to stay firm and sound convincing.

"Maybe not, but a few kisses never hurt anyone.

Besides, kissing you is infinitely better than just sitting around and sorting trash, which I know we have to do, but not every second."

Smiling, she shook her head. "Sit back and let's enjoy our drinks to celebrate that you discovered your real heritage. And it is something to celebrate, because it sounds to me as if it might be a whole lot better than being a Ralston with a dad you don't care about and a family feud you have to deal with."

She was right about that. He couldn't argue with her logic. But right now he was feeling anything but logical. Summoning the self-control that had kept him alive in Afghanistan, he forced himself to cool down and stop thinking about Emily's hot kisses and her soft, luscious body.

"It's difficult to get back to old letters with you so close," he said, "but I'll do my best."

"Good. We're on a tight schedule. I need to go back to what I was doing." Setting her glass on a table, she turned and he walked beside her to the door.

"Emily, I have something coming up on Saturday. It's a charity dinner dance in Dallas and I'm an honoree, so I have to attend. Will you come as my guest?"

She inhaled. "I'd love to," she answered smiling at him. "That's nice, Jake. What's the charity?"

"RAPT—Rescue A Pet Today. There are three of us being honored. After hurricanes that hit the

Louisiana and Texas Gulf coasts, we flew our own planes into flooded areas to pick up dogs that had been rescued to take them where they had a better chance at adoption. This was before I went into the service. They waited until we were all available to have this event in our honor."

"That's wonderful. Doug loves dogs. I'll tell him because that's one of his charities."

"I seriously doubt if there is anything I do that will impress your brother."

"That dog rescue will. Right now, I better get back to work." She stepped into the hallway, then turned back to look at him. "You know if we both used common sense, you wouldn't ask me to a dinner dance and I wouldn't go but..." She let the thought float there as she walked away.

Once again, Emily was right. If he'd used common sense, he wouldn't have asked her.

But common sense had vanished with their first kiss.

Lucas

Lucas combed his unruly hair that went right back into curls. He had a board meeting at their Kincaid Energy office, the family oil business, this afternoon, but right now he had another mission. He rubbed his clean-shaven jaw and glanced at himself. He was in a Western-style navy business suit, white dress shirt, navy tie and black boots. He intended to go next door and see if he could get a Ralston to speak to him.

He left his penthouse condo and walked around the corner to go into another office building and across the lobby to a small shop where a slender redhead was leaning over a jewelry counter.

She was concentrating on a tray of rings on the counter in front of her and his gaze traveled slowly over her. She had rosy cheeks, long dark red-brown eyelashes and long silky-looking red hair. Her creamy skin was flawless and beautiful. The dress she wore was some soft tan fabric that clung to her figure and revealed tempting curves, a tiny waist and then the counter hid the rest of the view of her. He had seen her moving around before and knew she had gorgeous long legs. Today she wore a gold bracelet and three rings on her fingers, but no engagement ring or wedding ring.

"Did you design all those?" he asked and she looked up. Her eyes were green, thickly lashed and beautiful.

"Yes," she answered, putting the tray below on a shelf. "I'm sorry, I was really concentrating. How may I help you?"

"I've seen your jewelry. You're talented."

"Thank you," she said, smiling with a flash of white teeth.

"I want to get my mother something pretty for

her birthday. Maybe a necklace. You do design necklaces, don't you?"

"Oh, yes. What does she like? Any color or type? Something formal or casual?"

"She likes old stuff and she has lots of jewelry. Just something pretty. You're wearing a pretty one," he said, glancing at a necklace around her slender neck. It was a gold medallion with a ring of diamonds near the center.

"I made this one and have another like it for sale."

"My mother has two grandkids now. It's probably so old-fashioned you won't have any, but do you have lockets? She had one with pictures of the grandkids but the necklace broke. Lockets might be out of style—at least I've never seen any except on my mom and my grandmother."

"Besides my originals that I create, I have antique jewelry. I have a few beautiful lockets. Just a minute."

She disappeared through a door that was only a few steps away, but it gave him a full view of her. She wore a short dress and his gaze swept down over long shapely legs, his pulse jumping. Her hair swung across her shoulders as she walked away. She was gorgeous and he wanted to take her out. He thought about the upcoming dinner dance honoring Jake that Doug had told him about. Would she go with him to honor a Ralston?

While he thought about how to ask Harper to go, she returned with two trays of jewelry that she placed on the counter.

"I bought these at estate sales, or from a family. None of these are new."

He looked at the lockets, but he couldn't ignore Harper's exotic perfume.

"Here's one," he said, pointing to a black locket, banded in gold with a diamond in the center.

She picked it up. "Good choice. This is onyx and that is solid gold and the diamond is one carat." She opened the locket.

"I think she would like that. How much is it?"

"I have the appraisal papers on it. It's over a hundred years old. The cost is $8,900.00. I can gift wrap it if you buy it."

"Do you like it?" he asked her, enjoying looking into her green eyes.

She smiled, a cheerful smile that made him want to hang around longer and get her to smile again. "Oh, yes. I don't buy anything I don't like."

"Harper, I want to buy that locket for my mother. Harper is your name, isn't it?"

"Yes, Harper Ralston."

"Glad to meet you, Harper Ralston," he said, offering his hand and shaking her warm, soft hand briefly when she held it out. "I want you to please gift wrap it and how about going next door to that new café with me for lunch? Can you get away?"

"For a short time," she said smiling. "And you are?"

"I didn't tell you on purpose. I'm Lucas Kincaid."

"A Kincaid?"

"Let me explain at lunch. Do you know a man named Thane Warner?"

She shook her head. "No, I don't. But a Ralston out to lunch with a Kincaid? That's a first in my life."

"I'll try to make sure you have a good time," he said, looking into her big green eyes while he smiled at her and she laughed, shaking her head.

"You're too good a customer to turn down."

"I'm just getting started," he said, lowering his voice. "I'm really not into that old feud much."

"Neither am I. So okay, Lucas Kincaid, you're on for lunch with a Ralston."

After she ate lunch on the go, Emily set out on the next item on her agenda. But first she had to get her tablet that she'd left in the bedroom she had taken for herself. Jake had the largest one that had a view of an area that could have once been a garden because of the dilapidated fences, trellises and statues. In her mind, she envisioned it after it was returned to its former glory.

But somehow that vision changed, morphing into her in Jake's embrace. Instead of flowering vines wrapping around wrought iron trellises, she saw his strong arms wrapping around her willing body. The heat she felt wasn't from the sun shining through the trees but from the desire he ignited in her. The—

Wait! What was she doing, allowing these erotic daydreams? Instantly she rubbed her eyes as if she could erase the sexy images. But every inch of her still tingled. What was it about Jake that made him irresistible? Whenever he touched her, desire filled her and logic and caution ceased to exist. She wanted to kiss him, to touch and hold him, to feel his marvelous body. At the same time, she didn't want to fall in love with him because he would never return the emotion.

When she took this job, she thought she'd grow immune to his charms. She hadn't expected to continue having this instant response to every physical contact with him. That hadn't ever happened with any other man in her life. But it had to stop. She had a job to do on the house and it was time to get back to work. Her best hope to get over Jake was to work as much and as quickly as possible.

She looked at the furniture she had already purchased. Her room had an antique four-poster bed, a tall chest with six deep drawers, a three-mirror vanity and a cheval mirror. All the furniture was solid mahogany and over one hundred years old, beautiful pieces that had been lovingly refinished.

She knew Jake was busy working in his office at the other end of the house so she took the opportunity to wander into his room next. The focal point of his bedroom was the four-poster oversize bed that had been handcrafted in the last century and had to have sheets made to fit because it was a foot longer and a foot wider than a king-size. It was covered with a dark blue duvet. All his furniture was solid maple, antique and professionally restored. She wandered into the modernized walk-in closet, looked out the old-fashioned windows and ran her fingers along the built-in bookcases.

"Ahh, were you going to surprise me?"

At the sound of his deep voice, she spun around to see Jake standing in the doorway, leaning against the jamb.

Instantly, a blush heated her cheeks. "No. I just wanted to see if your new furnishings looked satisfactory."

"I'd say you've done a bang-up job," he said in a deep voice, walking to her. With each step closer, her pulse accelerated and she could barely get her breath as she watched him.

"Jake, we just talked about this—"

"About what?" he asked, his eyes twinkling with mischief.

"About touching and kissing and not being businesslike at all."

He wrapped his arms around her waist and her

pulse drummed. "Darlin', we haven't been businesslike since the first hour we were together. If we weren't then, it'll never happen now. Too late. Too many hot kisses. You make me think of a lot of things, but neither business nor employer-employee relations come to mind."

"Jake, you're teasing," she said, trying to get some willpower and backbone and get out of his bedroom before he kissed her. "I'm getting out of here," she said.

"Without a kiss? Do you want to kiss? I do. You're a very sexy woman and I want to kiss you at least one more time today. It will make this whole day worth all the work."

She had to smile at that. "You're rotten. You know I can't resist you. We're piling up a bunch of trouble and I don't want a lot of heartache after I leave here."

He sobered and looked at her. "That does throw a cold blanket on hot kisses," he said quietly. "I don't want to hurt you. Okay, Emily, my darlin'. I'll see you at dinner tonight."

He stepped back, made a sweeping bow and held his hand in the direction of the open door. She got the message and left while she still could, fighting an intense urge to turn around, walk back into his arms and kiss him.

What was happening? He'd done what she wanted—he hadn't kissed her—yet, now she ached to be in his arms? She couldn't understand her own tangled feelings. No man had ever caused her this much trouble and longing the way Jake was. Her concentration was shot, which had never happened before, and that worried her. Jake was not the man to ensnare her thoughts and fill her with longing because he would never be serious and that's all she would ever be. If she fell in love with him, she would want marriage. Something he never wanted.

Shaking her head to banish the confusing thoughts and images, she forced herself to go back to work and appraise the many items they'd set aside. But the afternoon dragged.

They brought dinner in and she ate with Jake, just the two of them. Everyone else had gone to Flat Hill for the night and she was alone with Jake. He was charming, talking about his Hill Country ranch, his plans to settle there and how pretty it was, how different from this ranch. He invited her to come see it, but it was a casual invitation and she didn't think he would even remember it. He was entertaining, friendly and remote, and she got the sense he had decided to try to get their relationship back to business-only.

It was what she had wanted. Right?

During the week, Jake stuck to business and they both worked, trying to get things sorted— what he wanted to keep at the Long L Ranch, what he wanted to take with him to keep elsewhere and what he wanted disposed of.

After a week of working on the house and going through things, they flew back to Dallas on Friday night. She stopped by her parents' house to see them. They were gone, but Lucas was home.

"Mom left a note and said to hang around. They'll be home in an hour or thereabouts. They went to Dallas to shop. How's the old ranch?"

"We're changing the ranch house and it's going to look good. You should come see."

"Thanks. I'll pass on that. Doug and I guessed that you're going to the shindig tomorrow night to honor Jake."

"As a matter of fact, I am," she said, wondering whether Lucas would give her grief over her dinner date.

"Well, Jake did something good in rescuing the dogs and we figured you'd go. You know how we feel about rescue dogs, so Doug, Will and I reserved tables and we're taking friends."

Surprised, she smiled. "Thank you. That's really good news. Jake will be so pleased because he's trying to keep his promises to Thane and the biggest one was to try to end the Ralston-Kincaid feud."

Lucas faced her with his hands on his hips. "It's a cause we support, obviously, since we have rescue dogs. One more note to tell Jake on the subject of ending the feud—I invited a Ralston to go with me. Harper Ralston. She's a jewelry designer."

"Lucas, that is marvelous. Jake will really be pleased."

"Yeah, well, I didn't invite her to go with me to make Jake happy. I did decide to speak to her after your request that we try talking to Ralstons."

"I'll look forward to meeting her. I'm so pleased and I know Jake will be. He misses Thane and he's trying to do all he can."

"That's well and good, but—" he broke off and ran a hand through his blond hair "—Emily, be careful. You're seeing a guy who comes from a family that is totally dysfunctional and not one bit like ours. His mother has had four or five husbands."

"I know that and we're not serious, and I'm not going to be involved with his family."

Lucas shook his head. "I'm still warning you, watch out. Jake Ralston has a trail of broken hearts behind him and I don't want him to hurt you."

"There's nothing between me and Jake but a business deal and it's almost over. When it is, I'm sure he'll go out of my life."

"Doesn't sound as if he will since he's taking you to the big party and one that will honor him, so it's special to him. But I hope you're right. Just do yourself a favor and leave your heart at home on Saturday night."

"Thank you for the brotherly concern. I'll be okay and Jake will have a good time."

"Oh, I don't think you can find a woman who won't agree with you on that one. They still love him after he dumps them." Lucas threw up his hands. "I tried. Tell him if he hurts you, your brothers will beat him up."

"Lucas, don't—"

He laughed and shook his head. "I'm kidding. Well, you've been warned. I will let you cry on my shoulder and I'll restrain myself from saying I told you so."

She sighed and headed toward the door. "I'll call Mom and Dad. I have other things to do. As charming as your conversation is, I can tear myself away. See you at the party tomorrow night. Remember, Jake was a ranger, a friend of Thane's and he rescued a bunch of dogs."

"Yeah, yeah. A hero. And you remember what I said to you."

At the door, she turned. "I'm really glad you asked Harper Ralston. We're going to make a difference in the old feud. Thanks, Lucas."

"Sure. It was a sacrifice I made for you," he said, grinning, and she laughed.

"I can't wait to meet her," she said and left, laughing at her brother and knowing Jake would be pleased to hear another Ralston and Kincaid would be together at the party.

Lucas

Lucas walked to the window and watched his sister drive away. She was heading for heartache—he just knew it.

Jake Ralston had a reputation, a well-deserved reputation, judging from the women whose hearts he'd left broken. His MO had probably started from the time he was in high school. Doug and Jake were in the same classes, but Lucas had been in sports with Jake and knew the guy was intelligent, competitive and athletic. And a magnet for the females.

Lucas sighed and raked his fingers through his hair. He couldn't do anything about his sister. She'd never really been in love and usually was levelheaded, but some women seemed to lose all sense when it came to Jake. Lucas just hoped she didn't get hurt badly. At least Jake wasn't a marrying man, because as much as he wanted the feud to end, blending their two families would never work. With its history, Jake's was light-years removed from his and Emily's.

Lucas understood why she couldn't turn down Thane's million-dollar gift, but Lucas wished she wouldn't go Saturday night with Jake. "You're going to be another trophy, Sis," he said to the empty room. It wouldn't have done any good to have said that to Emily. She would do what she wanted to do regardless of what he said.

In the meantime, he had a date to get ready for. A date with Harper Ralston.

Saturday morning, Emily shopped and bought a new dress and shoes. Before noon, she got her hair styled, getting lighter blond highlights. Her long hair framed her face and the spiral curls fell over her shoulders.

Early in the evening, she dressed in a sleeveless red silk dress that had a low-cut V-neckline, a fitted waist and a straight skirt with a slit to her knee on one side. She felt bubbly excitement at the prospect of partying with Jake.

She had no idea what Jake really thought of her. She didn't spend time wondering because they had no future. She knew that she shouldn't have been going out with him and she shouldn't have gotten all dressed up for him if she intended to guard her heart, but temptation had been too great. She wanted a night to party with him and she wished for one night that he would really notice her. She knew he was aware of her in her sweatshirts and jeans, but for one evening, she longed for a few hours of fun with a handsome, sexy guy whose kisses could melt her. Tomorrow, she would return to life as usual and soon Jake would disappear from her life completely, so she was at least going to have one great memory.

She was certain they would see a lot of people they knew and therefore tonight should be another big blow to the Ralston-Kincaid feud. She thought about Jake not really being a Ralston. Only a handful of people knew that and none of them would reveal that secret, so tonight, to the world in this section of Texas, more than one Kincaid and a Ralston were out together, enjoying each other's company. They had worked long, hard hours on the ranch, way into the night, and she felt a growing eagerness to forget the tasks they still had to finish and simply enjoy the party with the handsome and sexy Jake.

The closer it got to six when he was picking her up, the more her excitement grew. She was ready and waiting when she heard a car and looked out to see a long white limo stop on her drive and Jake step out.

At the sight of him, her breath caught. He wore a white Stetson, a black tux with a white tux shirt, a black cummerbund and black boots. He looked gorgeous, a supersexy Texan.

She grabbed her small purse and hurried to the door. She shouldn't have been doing this, but one night shouldn't be life changing.

Seven

Jake went to the door in long strides. He had looked forward to this evening with Emily. He rang the bell and seconds later, she swung open the door. His gaze swept over her and he inhaled deeply while his heart hammered in his chest.

Stunned, he stared at her, for just a moment forgetting everything except Emily. The braid was gone. In its place was silky, shiny long blond hair with spiral curls and yellow highlights. Her rosy lips were redder, her lashes longer, darker. The V-neckline of her dress revealed her lush curves.

"You look gorgeous. Maybe I should just get a chair and sit here to look at you all evening. You're just so beautiful."

"Thank you, but no, you don't get a chair to sit here. I've been looking forward all day to a party. I have a new dress and shoes and we're not staying home."

"Yes, darlin', we'll go and have a very good time," he said, smiling. She was stunning. Why hadn't he seen this before? It was the same hair, the same eyes, the same lips, the same body, but all different. And her body—tonight she wasn't wearing the dumpy sweatshirt and baggy jeans and clothes that hid her curves. And what curves. He longed to touch them. His gaze followed the neckline of her red dress and he felt his heart race. How had he not seen this beneath the plain clothes, the lack of makeup, her hair secured in an ever-present braid?

"Jake?"

At the sound of her voice, he looked up and met her eyes. "What?"

"You're staring."

"Sorry. It's just… You're stunning."

"Thank you. I'm happy you noticed."

He smiled at her. "I promise, I noticed. Are you ready to go?"

"Oh, yes," she said, picking up her small purse. She locked up and he took her hand as they walked to the limo, where the chauffeur held the door and Jake helped her inside. Touching her even briefly, casually, made him want to pull her into his arms, hold her close and kiss her. Instead, he satisfied himself with sitting beside her.

"Thanks for inviting me, Jake. I feel privileged to be on the arm of the guest of honor."

He shrugged. "The rescue was something I could do easily. I like dogs and in storms like that they get lost and abandoned. Someone needs to look out for them."

"I'm glad you did."

"We can even get you a dog if you want to rescue one, but don't do it on an impulse because that doesn't work out sometimes."

She smiled. "I'll keep that in mind."

"Our tables are near the front. I have three tables of friends I've invited so I'll introduce you. Mike and Vivian will be there and so will Noah and Camilla and they'll be at our table."

"That's good because Vivian and Camilla and I can talk about art. And—surprise, surprise—Doug and Lydia took a table. Will took one, too. And I've saved the best for the last—Lucas took a table and here's the real surprise of the night—Lucas will be there with a Ralston."

"Wow. Thane knew how to reach people. That's amazing since Lucas was ready to slug me for being with you." Shaking his head, Jake laughed. "I'm glad to hear it."

"She's Harper Ralston. Do you know her?"

"No, but there are lots of Ralstons now and lots

of Kincaids. That was one reason I didn't think I could make a dent in the feud. That is good news about your brothers. I don't usually make enemies out of people I meet, but Doug and I go back to elementary school and competition in games at recess. With Lucas, I always figured it was more the old feud, and I barely know Will… I guess I'm doing better on my promises to Thane than I'd expected."

"I'm glad. I've given my family an incentive, remember?"

"Thane is going to get what he wanted and that makes me happy. I didn't think I could do anything about the feud beyond hiring you and I wasn't sure about that," Jake admitted.

But this whole time he was talking to her, he was only half thinking about her brothers, the feud and the dog rescue. He was thinking more about her and how much he wanted her all to himself.

He had looked forward to this night back with his ranger buddies and old friends, but now he wanted to skip the party and take her home with him and make love all night. He wanted to peel her out of that sexy red dress and kiss and hold her. He knew what they had done to each other in the past. Now it would be compounded by her fabulous looks. Could he get her to go home with him tonight? And if he did, would one night be enough?

Emily was the kind of woman who could complicate his life. She was picket fences and family dinners and forever. He didn't want to get into any kind of commitment.

He looked over at her and wondered just what trouble he was getting himself into with this woman.

They entered a big ballroom that had balloons around the room and tables around three sides that faced the stage and the dance floor. Propped on easels along two walls were posters of Jake and the two other honorees working with the dogs.

As they walked to their table, Jake constantly stopped to greet someone, introduce her and talk a minute. They were the first at their table, which was covered in crystal, glittering silver and centered with a vase of white orchids and red anthurium.

"This is beautiful, Jake," she said, aware of his hand lightly holding her forearm. She could detect the faint scent of his aftershave and it made her think of being alone with him later this evening.

"Ahh, here come the Grants and the Morettis," he said, calling her attention to the door.

"Vivian looks like a model," Emily said, looking at her blond friend who wore a black ankle-length dress that had a straight skirt, long sleeves and a deep V-neckline. She walked next to Mike, handsome in a black tux. "She doesn't even look pregnant yet. She doesn't show at all."

Walking beside them were Noah and Camilla. Camilla's long brown hair was straight and fell over her shoulders. She wore a deep blue ankle-length dress and greeted friends as they crossed the room.

Behind the two couples, Emily saw two of her brothers approaching. "Here come Doug and Lucas."

"Hi, Em. Congratulations, Jake," Lucas said, shaking Jake's hand.

"Congratulations and a big thank you," Doug said as he shook Jake's hand. "What you did was great. We haven't always agreed in the past—maybe never," he added, smiling, "but we agree on this. We came tonight because Lucas, Will and I all want to thank you for the dogs you helped rescue."

"It's good to find something we agree about," Jake said. "Thank you for taking tables. Everything helps."

"Yeah," Lucas said. "If you need us to help on one of the rescue missions, just let us know."

Jake smiled. "I'll remember that. It's good to know that some more Kincaids will work with a Ralston. That's what Thane wanted to have happen. I wish he could know it."

"Yeah, we can work with Ralstons. That's not impossible," Lucas said. "Sorry about your buddy. I know you and Thane were close."

"Thanks."

"Enjoy your evening," Doug said and walked away, and Jake faced Lucas, who had a sheepish grin.

"I guess I was hasty when we crossed paths in the lobby. This is a good charity and our family has nine rescue dogs. Em and I are the only ones without dogs. I'll send a check to this group."

"Thanks, Lucas."

"Well, enjoy your evening. I'll be sure to bring my date over to meet you. Do you know her, Jake? Harper Ralston?"

He shook his head. "But I'd like to meet her and I'm glad you invited her. That would really please Thane."

"Pleases me, too," Lucas said, grinning.

Jake watched Lucas walk away and shook his head. "Maybe we've found common ground. At least with your older brothers."

"Time will tell, but that was a good start," she said, turning to sit at the table to talk to Vivian and Camilla, who had her phone out and was showing Vivian pictures of Ethan. Emily asked to see and Camilla passed the phone to her. She looked at a smiling little boy with thick black curls and blue eyes. "He looks like Noah."

"Yes, he does. They're having fun with each other. Noah's a great dad."

"Mike, Noah and Jake," Vivian said, "they're great guys. And so was Thane."

"Vivian, I'm grateful to Thane and you for your

generosity. You could have gotten the old ranch house cleaned up and everything cleared out of it without giving me such a generous gift."

"I'm excited for you," Vivian said to Emily. "Thane really wanted that feud to end because it caused him trouble sometimes. I know he was trying to keep Mike from having to deal with fighting neighbors. Anyway, you and Camilla and I will be able to work together on our art." She turned to Camilla. "When our baby comes, I'll probably call you with questions."

"Any time," Camilla answered.

Vivian looked at Emily. "I'm glad Jake is happy with the Long L Ranch because no one in our family wanted it. Thane didn't intend to keep it. I didn't want it and neither does Mike. He runs our ranch and isn't interested in another."

"I didn't want the Long L Ranch, either," Camilla said. "Thane asked me if I did and I told him I never wanted to set foot on it again."

"I don't know whether Jake will ever live there, but it isn't going to look like it did," Emily explained. "While he's keeping some things, I don't think you'll recognize the place when he's through doing it over."

"It was a creepy old place and I hated going there," Camilla said. "I wouldn't want Ethan there at all. It was scary."

"It won't be scary, I promise you," Emily said.

"I'm glad Jake is changing it. I hope he likes it. None of us did, but that was because of our grand-father. Not the most lovable old granddad. And none of us liked going to that ranch after our little brother drowned in a pond there," Camilla added.

"That is a bad memory," Emily agreed. "But I hope you can stand to come look when it's fin-ished. You'll be surprised."

"You might have to send pictures, Emily. I can't imagine going back there ever," Camilla repeated.

Jake sat beside Emily. "They're getting ready to start serving," he said. As he spoke, the first waiters came out of the kitchen with large trays. In minutes, waiters poured drinks and served crystal plates with green salads.

After a dinner of prime rib and a delicious lemon dessert, the program started. A short film was shown of the rescue flights that were made and the director of RAPT talked, giving figures for the number of dogs that had been placed in homes. Jake, along with two other Texans, were given plaques, honoring what they had done in flying the dogs out of the disaster areas.

Finally, the evening was turned over to a band for dancing and a bar opened in one corner of the room.

The dancing was lively and Emily had fun with Jake. Not surprisingly, he was a superb dancer, no matter the style—samba, salsa, rumba. She liked watching Jake and his sexy moves. Longing built with every dance, every shared laugh, but she refused to worry about it tonight.

Later, when they played a ballad, Jake took her hand to slow dance. "You can't beat this. Slow dancing may be old-fashioned, but I get to hold you close. Even better, your brothers and their lady friends have gone, so I won't be getting the evil eye for it."

"Pay no attention to my brothers. Frankly, I don't imagine they want to mess with you. You've had military training—they haven't."

"I may have training, but I didn't come home to fight any Texans I've known all my life. And it would go against my promise to Thane."

"It will never come to that now," she said, aware of being in Jake's arms, moving with him. His hand holding hers was warm; his arm circled her waist and they moved together in perfect harmony. She looked up into his eyes and as he gazed back at her, the moment changed. His arm tightened slightly around her waist and she longed to press even closer.

"We fit together perfectly," he said quietly.

"I think so," she whispered, looking at his mouth, feeling her heart beat loudly as she followed his lead. He spun her around and dipped and she clung to him as she looked up at him. He held her easily and swung her up to pull her close. The song ended and another started, a jazz number, and the more they danced, the more she wanted to be alone with him, kissing him to her heart's content. Her pulse raced, desire building with every step she took.

When the song was over, he whispered in her ear. "Ready to go?"

"Yes," she whispered back.

He took her hand and they walked back to their table, where she picked up her purse and they told everyone goodbye.

In the limo, Jake took her hand. "Emily, come back to my place for a drink. I'll take you home whenever you're ready. It's early and it's been a fun evening. I'm not ready for it to end yet."

After only a moment's hesitation, she replied, "Yes."

He smiled. "Good."

She knew she shouldn't, but she didn't want to say good-night to him yet, either. The evening had been great fun with Jake and with friends. It had been all she had hoped and more because of Jake and now she could no longer ignore how much she wanted to kiss him and be kissed by him. But could she stop at kisses? Did she even want to?

Eight

They rode up in the elevator to his condo. When she walked into the entryway and looked across the living room, through floor-to-ceiling windows, she could see the Dallas skyline.

"What would you like to drink? I have a full bar."

"Surprise me. You also have the best view in Dallas," she said, crossing his living room, which had ornate French Louis XV fruitwood furniture. The furnishings were elegant, with a spectacular crystal chandelier in the entryway and another in the dining room just as it had looked in the pictures he had given her. She knew his kitchen was contemporary style.

She stood at the window to take in the panoramic view, including Reunion Tower, the Dallas skyline and twinkling city lights. While looking in wonder, she was lost in memories of dancing with him. All the touching and caressing had been pure seduction. But now she reminded herself she needed to get a grip on reality and guard her heart. No matter how appealing, how sexy, how much they had this fiery physical attraction to each other, they needed to exercise common sense and keep their distance. She needed to hang on to that thought as if it was a lifeline. Otherwise, she was going to fall in love with him and that would be a giant disaster.

Why couldn't she get that through her head and walk away from Jake? He was just too appealing, and they had a sizzling chemistry between them that was pure magic.

So what was she doing in his condo? Why was she hot, tingling with wanting him?

Because she wanted this night with him. As dangerous as it was.

"Jake?" she whispered.

He approached her with two glasses of wine. When he looked at her, his eyes narrowed and he set the glasses on the nearest table, shed his coat, unbuttoned his shirt at the throat and pulled loose his tie. As she watched, her heartbeat quickened. Dropping his tie on the chair, he closed the distance between them and took her into his arms.

While her breathing quickened, her pulse was a drumbeat in her ears. She wanted him with all her being. At the moment she didn't give a thought about caution or risking her heart. She didn't care about the future. All she knew was being in Jake's embrace.

He wrapped his arms around her, looked into her eyes and brushed her lips with his.

Clinging to him, holding him tightly, she moaned softly as she opened her mouth to him, meeting his tongue with her own. Sensations swept her and she thrust her hips against him.

"Jake," she whispered. His name was all she could manage.

"We've been heading here since the day we met. You're gorgeous, Emily. I want to kiss you, to hold you, to touch you everywhere, to look at you. But I respect what you want. I told you I would get you home whenever you wanted. If you want to stop and go home, you tell me," he whispered, brushing light kisses on her throat and her ear before raising his head to look into her eyes.

He was giving her a chance to walk away.

"Tonight, I want to be in your arms. I want to kiss you and I want you to kiss me. We have something special between us."

"Do we ever," he whispered. He tightened his arms around her, leaned over her and placed his mouth on hers in a hot kiss that consumed her and caused a sizzling response that was a thousand times greater than ever before. She moaned with longing, with desire, wanting his mouth and his hands all over her, wanting his energy and strength funneled to her, wanting to touch and discover him.

She closed her eyes, letting her tongue stroke his, running her fingers in his thick hair.

Breaking the kiss, he straightened, and she opened her eyes to see his heated gaze meet hers as he reached around her and unzipped her dress, pushing her red silk dress off her shoulders while he trailed kisses on her ear and on her throat.

"You were gorgeous tonight. Absolutely beautiful. And I will always remember when you opened the door and I first saw you." He brushed kisses lower and pushed her dress off her hips and it fell with a swish around her ankles. She stepped out of it as he unfastened her bra and tossed it away. When he cupped her breasts with his warm hands, she gasped with pleasure, closing her eyes, giving herself over to the sensation, letting Jake stroke and caress and kiss her breasts, first one and then the other while he murmured how beautiful she was. She knew she was headed for heartache because this was casual to Jake. Their intimacy would carry no meaning to him, nothing lasting, while to her, every caress was thrilling, each touch was exciting. Even the lightest kiss created a bond.

She wanted a sharing of bodies and lovemaking, a union. The difference between them was—she wanted it over a lifetime. She wanted the promises, the vows and the commitment, and he never would.

She had to make love on his terms, or walk away now and never know the fullness of Jake's passion.

He took her nipple in his mouth and with one suckle she knew her answer.

She placed her hands on both sides of his face, turning him to look into his eyes, and then she pulled his head closer and kissed him with a deliberation that she hoped conveyed all the longing and need in her.

As they kissed, he wrapped her in his arms, picking her up.

Her heart pounded and her body burned with desire. She longed to kiss him from head to toe and discover his marvelous, strong male body. He was in prime shape, obviously, carrying her easily as he went to his bedroom, yanked the duvet off the bed and stood her on her feet.

"You are so beautiful," he whispered, cupping her breasts and running his thumbs over her nipples. She gasped as she began to peel away his shirt, then unfastened his trousers.

He jerked off his cummerbund and tossed it. Watching her, he pulled off his boots, socks, then finally his briefs, freeing him. He was aroused, his shaft hard and ready. He had a sprinkling of curly black hair across his chest, and she ran her fingers through the crisp curls and then leaned closer to rub her breasts against him while she stepped out of her high heels and kicked them away. As she peeled off her lacy panties and tossed them, she heard his deep intake of breath.

He held her with his hands splayed on her hips. "You don't know what you do to me. I want to take all night to touch and kiss every inch of you. I want you with me tonight. I want you with me this weekend."

Before she could answer, he kissed her, pulling her warm naked body against his. Desire rocked her and she wanted him to make love to her. She wanted him to fill her, to be inside her, to be one with her.

She ran her hands over him. He was all hard muscle, in prime condition, his erection thick and ready for her.

He picked her up, placed her on his bed and knelt beside her to run his hands over her legs so slowly while he trailed kisses on her body. Moving between her legs, he ran the tip of his tongue up the inside of her legs, kissing her behind her knees, moving up, his tongue, wet and warm, trailing along the inside of her thigh as he watched her.

Closing her eyes, she gasped with pleasure,

wanting him while she arched her hips. His fingers moved between her legs, to stroke and caress her. "You're perfect," he whispered. She gasped and shifted beneath his touch, wanting him while he drove her to want more. Clutching his arms that were rock-hard with muscle, she clung to him, wanting him inside her as he stroked her and coaxed her to the point of no return.

"Jake, I need you," she cried and sat up, wrapping her arms around him to draw him closer to kiss him.

He slipped his arm around her waist, holding her and kissing her while his other hand played lightly over her, caressing her inner thighs and between her legs.

"I want you to make love to me," she whispered.

"Don't rush us," he answered in a hoarse voice. "Let me make it as good as possible for you."

She pushed him down on the bed to move over him. "Let me do the same," she whispered as she straddled him, her tongue teasing his nipples, drifting down over his belly to the inside of his thighs while she wrapped her hand lightly around his thick rod to caress and stroke him.

As she caressed him, he gasped and clenched his fists. She closed her hand lightly around his thick staff again while she ran her tongue over him, stroking him slowly. Her hands played over him as her tongue circled the velvet tip of his manhood.

She took him in her mouth and suddenly he sat up, turning and placing her on the bed and stepping away to open a drawer and get a packet.

As he moved between her legs to put on a condom, she held out her arms. With all her being, she wanted him to make love to her. She didn't have to think, only feel, but she knew she was in love with him. She was equally certain she would get hurt, but tonight, even though it would cause her pain later, she longed for his loving and his marvelous, sexy male body.

She felt this was a once-in-a-lifetime for her. So be it. She would never again know a man like Jake.

As he lowered himself, she spread her legs, wrapping them around his slender hips. She held him with her arms around him and he kissed her, his tongue going deep.

With her eyes closed tightly, she ran her fingers down his smooth back, down over his hard buns and the back of his thighs with their short, crisp hairs, while sensations bombarded her.

He entered her slowly, so slowly, and withdrew to enter her again. Gasping, she arched against him. Desiring him more with each drawn-out stroke, she held him tightly.

He continued thrusting, filling her slowly and withdrawing, and she matched his rhythm as she'd done when they'd danced that evening.

"Jake, love me," she whispered, running her

hands over him, trying to pull him closer so he would go deeper.

But he kept his control. "I want to pleasure you until you faint with ecstasy," he whispered, running his tongue over the curve of her ear.

"Jake," she cried out, clinging to him, moving faster against him.

Finally, his control was gone. When he pumped faster, harder, she moved with him, feeling a blinding need that built while she lost awareness of everything else and thrashed beneath him. She raised her hips, moving wildly as she climaxed with an intense orgasm that shot through her, hot, blinding, causing a roaring in her ears. Sensations rocked her and perspiration covered her while she cried out with rapture.

Pumping wildly, Jake's control vanished. They moved together with her climaxing again only seconds before Jake.

Gradually, they slowed. He was covered with sweat, still holding her with his arms under her. He let his weight down, turned on his side, keeping her with him.

She held him, opening her eyes when he showered her face with light kisses.

"You're fantastic," he whispered. "Absolutely fantastic." He brushed damp locks of blond hair away from her face, caressing her.

"You're beautiful. You're also the sexiest woman I've ever known," he whispered.

"You must tell them all that because there is no way I'm the sexiest woman in your life."

He raised up, propping his head on his hand to look at her as he continued to lightly comb long strands of her hair from her face. "Emily, you're fantastic and tonight has been marvelous," he said.

She smiled, running her fingers over his face, feeling the prickly stubble on his jaw and chin. His hair was tangled on his forehead.

"Move into my bedroom with me," he whispered. "I want more than just working with you on the ranch and going to our own rooms at night. We could have magic nights. Magic days, too. We'll be alone on the Long L Ranch at night."

"Jake, tonight was an exception."

He kissed her and stopped her talking. For an instant, she was tempted to wiggle away and tell him that she wouldn't move in with him, but when she wiggled or even just tried to move a fraction, his arms tightened around her and he held her close.

"I don't want to let you go, not tonight, not tomorrow. When I do, I want to know I can get you back," he whispered. He leaned back to look at her. "Will you stay with me in my room this week? Give us this week together, Emily."

"I wasn't going to do this. The longer we're together, the more it'll hurt when we part."

"I don't think so," he whispered, shifting slightly and running his hand over her hip and along her thigh.

The slightest touch stirred desire again. She thought if they kissed and made love, she would be satisfied and have enough memories to walk away with her heart relatively intact. Now she didn't think so. She suspected that the more involved she was with him, the more it was going to hurt to say goodbye. And she would say goodbye.

She turned on her side to look at him and placed her hand on his jaw. "Tonight was special, very special."

"Yes, it was and I don't want it to end," he agreed, twisting long locks of her hair in his fingers.

"There have been few men in my life," she said, giving him a long look. "If we're together in bed a lot more, I'll fall deeply in love with you. We had tonight. That's it. I have to step back to avoid a broken heart because you and I don't fit together. We really don't fit—not our lifestyles, not our families, not our backgrounds. You don't want marriage, a family, kids. I do."

He shook his head. "I can't change. My family's track record on commitment is lousy. And you know the secret we found, which just complicates the relationships that much more."

"Let's get the house fixed and say goodbye," she said.

"I promise you, it'll be easy to walk away because you wouldn't want to marry me, even if I wanted to."

"No, I wouldn't because it couldn't work out. Tonight is special. I'll stay here with you tonight and then we forget this happened."

He caught her chin in his fingers, which were warm, gentle, and as he gazed into her eyes, her heart drummed so much she thought he would hear its beating.

"There's no way to forget you. I can't make this permanent and you wouldn't say yes if I asked, but I'll never forget tonight. From that first handshake, our relationship has been intense, like a simmering volcano. I've never had reactions to any other woman the way I have to you, and you said you haven't with any other man."

"That's right. That's why I wanted tonight, Jake," she said, combing his thick wavy black hair off his forehead with her fingers, watching it fall right back. He looked disheveled, strong, sexy, and she was beginning to want his arms around her and his mouth on hers again. Why was she so attracted to him? Instead of getting him out of her system, making love tonight had only increased the attraction.

She had feared that would happen, but she'd wanted a night with him, anyway. At least she was trying to resist temptation and use some judgment and wisdom. On the ranch, if she spent each night in his bed, in his arms until they finished the job, she would be so in love with him, she couldn't imagine saying goodbye, but he would walk out and never look back.

He would leave her with a broken heart that would never mend.

"I wasn't even going to stay here tonight," she said. "If we make love every night, I'll never get over it. You're incredibly sexy, Jake. We have something sparking between us that keeps us attracted to each other. We can work well together and play well together. In short, you're desirable and I need to back off before you have my heart locked away and I can never get over you or marry anyone else. Maybe if we just started planning a wedding, you would cool down and forget about another night together."

"Ahh, Emily. I can't laugh about it."

"I wasn't being funny. If I start talking about a wedding, you'll run."

"I might not. You're not going to want a wedding and I know it. You wouldn't say yes if I gave you a twenty-carat diamond now and got down on my knee and proposed."

They looked at each other and she hurt. "You're right. I wouldn't. I know you won't propose, but you're right. You're not the man for me and my family, who are together constantly."

He wrapped her in his arms and pulled her close against him, their naked bodies pressed tightly together, her leg over his as she held him. She could feel his heart beating. He was warm, solid, muscled and so great in so many ways, but not in the ways that she wanted in a husband. That wasn't possible. He would never fit into her family and he would never want to. And he didn't want to be a dad and he might not know how.

She was wrapped in his arms, in intimacy and sated by hot sex that had fully pleasured them both, but it had to end and they had to part.

The sooner they did, the less it would hurt. Getting over one night together would not be monumental.

Says who?

The nagging small voice wasted no time in questioning her. And she was forced to listen. No other man she had known was like Jake or had held the appeal for her that he did—the instant chemistry with any slight physical contact.

The silence spread between them and she couldn't find words to change the situation. They didn't have a future together. Tonight was all she could have with him.

She clung to him and wondered how long her memory of this night would last. How long would she want to look back on this night with him when it would hurt so badly? He was so much that was wonderful, but the basic essential ingredient was missing. He was right. If he proposed now, she would say no.

She turned to ask him, "Jake, you'll never care about a family, will you?"

He smiled as he shook his head. "No, I don't think I will. That isn't my life and not the way I grew up. Sorry, Emily. For that, you have the wrong guy. But," he said, drawing her close in his embrace, "we can still have a lot of fun and enjoy each other and be friends. That's a lot."

Even though it hurt, she smiled at him. "I suppose it is and it's all we're going to have. Tonight together."

"Maybe I can change your mind on that one. Sure, you don't want to try to win me over to your way of viewing things?" he teased, and she laughed and just for tonight let go of concerns about the future. She was with him and she was going to enjoy him, relish in the discovery of his marvelous body and revel in the most fantastic sex ever.

"Let me show you my shower," he said, breaking into her thoughts. "It's a cut above the new one they put in downstairs at the Long L."

"Hey, I selected that ranch shower and it was expensive. It's new, fancy and quite spiffy. What don't you like about it?"

"Calm down. It's fine for the ranch. But this is where I spend a lot of my time, so here, I have the deluxe. I have just what I want," he said, getting out of bed and picking her up easily to carry her to his bathroom. "I'll show you." He looked at her intently. "You're beautiful," he said, his voice dropping and sounding husky. "I like this."

She slipped her arms around his neck and smiled at him. "I like it, too. I like it a lot," she whispered. She ran her fingers in his hair at the back of his head and closed her eyes to kiss him. He stopped walking and kissed her in return, his tongue stroking her, going deep into her mouth. Her eyes were closed, her pulse racing as she clung to him, and she knew this was a time she would remember all her life.

"Jake," she whispered, opening her eyes to look at him and remind him where they were heading. "Shower?"

He carried her into an en suite with two areas, one with vanities, sinks, a commode, chairs, a large-screen TV and potted palms. On the other side of a marble knee wall was another large area with mirrors along one wall, a vanity on another, a round sunken tub in the middle and a huge glass shower.

"Oh, my word, you could get lost in here," she said, laughing at the size of his bathroom. "You'll really be roughing it at the ranch, and I thought I was getting luxurious bathrooms for you there."

He stood her on her feet in the large shower and turned on jets of warm water and soon they were kissing while he ran his hands over her and she caressed him.

He turned off the water and got a thick towel, handing one to her and taking another as he turned to dry her with light teasing strokes that made her want to toss the towel and make love where they stood. They dried each other and in minutes, he crossed the room to open a drawer and returned with a condom, which he put on while she kissed him. His skin was damp, warm, and she ran her hands over his body. He was hard, ready to love.

His brown eyes were dark with desire. He cupped her breasts, leaning down to kiss first one and then the other. She held his upper arms and closed her eyes as he circled each nipple with his thumb and forefinger. Moaning softly, stepping closer to slip her arm around his neck, she stood on tiptoe to kiss him.

As they kissed, his hands closed on her waist and he lifted her. She clung to him, wrapped her arms around his neck and her legs around his hips, sliding down slowly while he entered her.

She gasped with pleasure, moving on him. He thrust into her and in minutes they rocked together fast, until she climaxed, crying out and clinging to him while ecstasy enveloped her.

Jake pumped wildly, bringing her to a second climax as he thrust hard and deep and reached his own release.

He kissed her, a slow, hungry kiss that was also confirmation of exciting, mind-blowing sex.

In minutes when their breathing slowed, he carried her back into the shower to turn on warm sprays of water. After they dried, he picked her up again. "I like this, you in my arms, pressing against me so warm and soft while both of us are nude." His voice was husky, sexy and the look in his eyes made her tingle.

He carried her back to bed with him to hold her stretched close against his side. "I don't want to let you go," he said.

"You don't have to let me go for the next hour for sure. I don't think I can stand up by myself," she said, feeling blissful.

"Would you believe me if I told you that you're the first woman I've ever brought up here?"

Startled, she looked at him. "No, I wouldn't. You're in magazines and society pages with gorgeous women. Are you trying to tell me you have never taken one home with you?"

"Not to this condo. That's exactly what I'm telling you. I don't bring them here or take them to my ranch. I'm a very good customer of one of the hotels here and I book a penthouse suite often because it's convenient and where I take a woman if I bring anyone with me after a night out. Usually I'm at their place because then I can leave when I want. You're the first to stay in my condo."

She laughed. "I'm surprised and I would guess you brought me to your inner sanctum either because it was the easiest thing to do or because you know I'm not going to hunt you down or bother you later."

He rolled on his side to look at her, playing with locks of her long hair. "Darlin', you can come here anytime you want and I'll be glad to see you. If you'd like to visit my Hill Country ranch, I'll take you to visit. You're welcome there."

"That's very kind, Jake. I'm flattered, I suppose, but I don't think we really have a future together. I also don't think you'd tell me if you knew I would come see you. Besides, I'd rather not think about that tonight. Goodbyes will come soon enough."

"Don't write me off so fast, Emily."

"My goodness, that sounds like a man who is contemplating a commitment." She feigned exaggerated surprise.

"Don't read that into anything I've said, because I haven't changed," he said, suddenly sounding serious. She suspected he was and she needed to stick to her plan to tell him goodbye and go on her way. Because for Jake, commitment was a four-letter word.

But not now. For now, she let him pull her closer against him, and she turned on her side, her leg over his, her arm across his chest as she held him, content to lie with him.

"See, Jake," she murmured, "this is what I want in my life, constant nights like this, spectacular sex and then just being with a special person every night possible."

"Are you giving me a sales pitch?"

She smiled. "No. I'm explaining how I feel because you don't comprehend that. You like coming home to an empty condo—you don't bring anyone home with you. Ditto to your ranch. You like your solitude, your single life, your freedom—although it's freedom from love and family and a lot of good things, so I wouldn't label it *freedom*. Anyway, we don't feel the same about how we live."

"I know what we do feel the same about," he said, nuzzling her neck and then running his tongue over the curve of her ear and trailing light kisses to her mouth. She rolled over into his arms and gave herself to his kiss, and conversation ended.

* * *

It was midmorning when Jake stirred, turned on his side to wrap his arms around Emily and brushed light kisses on her shoulder. She turned to him, coming awake. They had made love all through the night. He couldn't get enough of her and, from what she'd said last night, this might be the one and only time he would get to be with her like this. If any other woman he had known had given him the same speech last night that Emily had, about one night only, he would have dismissed it as something he could change her mind about, but he hadn't with Emily. She had a streak in her that made him feel she meant what she said and she'd have the willpower to stick with it.

She could settle for one night of love, but he didn't want to. She had rocked his world and he wasn't ready to see her walk out of it. And that alone was a first for him.

She had been stunning to look at last night and sex with Emily was all he had hoped for and more. How could she dazzle him in bed when she was so inexperienced, so down-to-earth practical? He'd been trying, unsuccessfully, to figure her out from the first few minutes they had met. He couldn't understand why they had such a fiery chemistry between them. She was a puzzle in several ways, but one thing he was sure of. Even though he couldn't meet her terms—marriage and total commitment—he wanted more than just last night with her.

He kissed her awake and they made love again and showered again and had sex again. He felt he was in paradise and he hoped she would spend the weekend with him.

It was late Sunday afternoon when she sat up. "Jake, it's ten minutes after three," she said, sounding breathless while she looked down at him and frowned.

"Time for love," he drawled and pulled her down. She opened her mouth to protest and he covered her mouth with his, kissing her until she wrapped her slender arms around him and kissed him in return.

Finally, she wiggled away and sat up. "Jake, my family will be getting together at my parents' house at five. I need to be there. I don't want them asking questions about where I've been because I'm always truthful."

"Just tell them you went home with me and the sex was so good, that we lost track of time. Stick to the truth."

"I'm not telling them I went home with you."

"I don't mind."

"I'll bet you don't."

He laughed and pulled her into his arms. "We'll get dressed. I'll get my pilot to have the plane ready. We'll fly back to the ranch and before we leave Dallas, you call and tell your mom that you won't be home for dinner tonight because we needed to get back to the ranch."

"I suppose that's as good as I can do. Very well. I'll get ready to go."

"I'll take you home so you can get your things," he said and got up. When she stepped out of bed, he picked her up.

"We do have time for one more shower."

"Oh, Jake." He kissed her then, continuing until he stepped into his shower, stood her on her feet and turned on sprays of warm water again.

"I hope you had more fun being here with me than you would have had with your brothers if you had gone home."

"You know I have, but I'll get all sorts of arguments from my brothers and dire warnings about spending time with you."

"And do you have regrets?" Jake asked, tilting her chin up to look into her eyes. "Do you?"

Nine

She looked into his dark brown eyes and shook her head. "I should have," she whispered.

But she didn't.

By the time they finished showering, Jake carried her back to bed to kiss her from head to toe.

Later, she snuggled against him. "I need to go home, get my things and we'll fly back to the ranch as I told my family. I'm not staying here in your condo tonight."

"I know we're not. We'll go now and get your things and leave for the ranch. You'll be there before seven o'clock. Come on. You take this bathroom and shower, and I'll take one of the others," he said, getting out of bed and moving around.

She watched him, her gaze drifting down over him, and desire ignited within her. His body was enticing, muscled, fit and strong. He looked marvelous and she wanted to walk back into his arms and make love again and again through the night.

He turned and saw her staring at him. His chest expanded as he inhaled deeply. "Emily—"

"Go on, Jake. We have to go," she said quickly, blushing as she turned and grabbed up clothes, hurrying to his bathroom without looking back.

Jake's pulse raced as he headed to another shower. A cold shower this time. He'd noticed how she studied him. One look at her eyes and it was obvious she was ready to make love again. And, therefore, now he was. Emily was as insatiable as he was. His heart pounded and he wanted to turn around and hurry back to join her in the shower. How he would have liked to stay here tonight and keep making love. They could do the same at the ranch, but she might change her mind by then. Reason and work might interfere and she would refuse.

Instead of getting enough of making love with her, he wanted more. The more they had sex, the more he wanted to have sex with her.

His thoughts weren't helping. He needed to think about something besides Emily's naked body in his bed.

"Oh, damn," he said softly. How could she tie him up in knots like this after they had made love all weekend? No woman had ever done that, especially one that waxed on about commitment and family, one that wanted marriage and love.

He was not in love. And he never would be. That was just impossible.

An hour later they were airborne, leaving Dallas, and she wondered whether she had had the most wonderful weekend of her life or something she would forever look back on and wish she had done differently.

Shooing those thoughts out of her mind, she spent the flight going over what was left for her to do at the Long L. She thought she could finish up at the ranch in two weeks, possibly sooner.

In a short time, they landed and were driven in a limo to the ranch. Finally, they were alone in the big ranch house and Jake walked over to put his hands on her waist.

"On the plane when we talked, you said you can wind up what you have to do out here in two weeks."

"Yes, if not sooner," she said. "The painters should be done with the upper floors this week or next. When the workmen redo the floors upstairs, the place will have to be empty because of the fumes, so we'll all have to be out at that time.

In the meantime, I'll select furniture and work with the decorator."

"Okay, so there's maybe two weeks we'll be together, Emily," he said in that deep, coaxing voice that made shivers run up her spine. "Move into my suite these last two weeks. This probably will be the last time in our lives we'll be together and I want you with me before you go out of my life forever. I want memories because you're incredibly special. I can't even weigh the pros and cons of marriage and consider if I should propose, because I know right now if I do, you'll say no." He leaned closer and looked deeply into her eyes.

"Emily, am I right? If I propose, you'll say no?"

His question made her ache and long for a different answer while she looked into his dark brown eyes that became almost black with passion. "Ahh, Jake. We just weren't meant to be. Would you want to do all the family things? Would you want to spend every Sunday night with family? My family— Doug, Lucas, Will, Andrea, the little kids, Mom and Dad, grandparents? Do you want half a dozen kids? Do you want one?"

"I don't know how to be a good dad. Mine were lousy. I don't know how to do any of those family things and no, I wouldn't want to spend Sunday nights with your brothers, although they have become more civil to me. No, you're right. You and I have no future together. I can't be the husband you want and I don't really want a wife. I don't want the responsibility of a family. So there you are. We may have no future but we have whatever time you're here. Darlin', move in with me for these last two weeks on the ranch. I need some good memories and so do you. Okay?"

Again, another question from him gave her pause. This one was easier to answer. She knew she was going to get hurt in the worst way, be so lost when he disappeared from her life. It was too late now, anyway, because she was already in love with him. How much more would a week or two make it hurt when they parted? She wanted the memories and she wanted him.

"I will if you'll go to one Sunday night dinner at home with me. Jake, you don't even know what family is all about."

"Well, I sort of do, from when I was a kid and would go home with Thane. His family is probably a lot like yours. All buzzing around each other like a swarm of bees. They were nice and it was fun to be at his house, I'll admit. Sure, I'll trade one Sunday dinner for two weeks with you in my bed. That's a deal, darlin'. We start tonight." He took her notebook from her hands to set it aside and then he turned around to look at her. "You're through working for tonight because I want you in my arms, in my bed all night long."

She slipped her arms around his neck, kissing him, holding him tightly. She hadn't thought through her answer, she just went with the gut feeling of what she wanted to do. Stay in his bed.

She was going to miss him terribly and he would tear up her heart and smash it into little pieces when he said goodbye. Each hour they were together, she loved him more, but she wasn't going to tell him that and she didn't want him to know.

She would have two weeks of paradise before he said goodbye and she really didn't think she would see him again after that. And he was right, if he proposed to her, she would say no. He wouldn't want to be around family. He wouldn't want to be a dad. He just wasn't the man for her—if only her body could get that. When they were so different, why did they have this huge sizzling attraction for each other? And when they were such opposites, why did they like being together?

Ordinary life could be a giant mystery sometimes and this was one of those times. She couldn't explain Jake. She just had to get over him.

One afternoon at the end of the first week, Jake tossed down his pen and stopped trying to concentrate on some letters he needed to answer. He couldn't get Emily out of his thoughts. Or her words about them being complete opposites. She was right. They were 180 degrees apart on topics like love, marriage and family.

Her sister was married. None of his siblings were married now. Everyone in his family had had disastrous relationships and they weren't a close family. Hers was together constantly with strong ties, the proverbial one big happy family. He couldn't even imagine that life.

His brothers had been convincing in their condemnation of matrimony and warnings about it. Jake didn't think he'd ever take the plunge but Emily wanted marriage.

Yes, it was obvious they were not meant for each other—he had known that from the first hour with her and was always reminded of it when he was with her.

He needed to walk away and forget her.

The minute that thought came, another thought followed it—he had never had sex with anyone else who was as exciting, fiery and unforgettable as Emily was. Of all the women he had known, he had to find the hottest sex ever with the one woman who not only wanted a wedding ring but also a guy who would become a total family man—friendly with in-laws, great with kids, happy having relatives around, even raising dogs. Ties and responsibility and a cluster of family were just not meant for him. So why couldn't he shake her out of his thoughts? Why couldn't he get enough of being with her?

She had one more week after this one at the

Long L Ranch and then she would be finished staying on the ranch. She would come back for furniture deliveries and to work with the decorator, but she wouldn't be staying or flying back and forth with him.

He knew she was working late, getting up early, had three assistants to help her finish as fast as possible and he suspected it was to get away from him.

They were logical, straightforward and realistic about their relationship until about five every afternoon. Then he underwent a transformation that made him wonder about himself. She did, too. All day they worked hard to get through with the things left in the house, to clear out what he didn't want. At about five o'clock, he knew the dinner hour approached and after dinner they might work a little, but around eight o'clock, she would join him in his bedroom. From that time on, they were in each other's arms for fiery kisses, blazing sex and a night of love.

They each knew their time together was limited and she seemed as determined as he was to make every night a memory. He wondered if any other woman would ever appeal to him the way Emily did. He hoped so, because he and Emily had no future together. He didn't even want to think about that one.

Sunday he had promised to go home with her

if she would spend these nights in his bed, so he had to honor his promise. He wondered whether her brothers would be as friendly as they had been at the charity dinner.

When they left the company of her family Sunday night, she planned to stay at her house and he would stay at his condo. Monday morning they would fly back to the ranch. On Saturday of that week, she expected to finish the job and move out and he wouldn't see her after that, except a day or two for furniture deliveries. They had already talked about it several times and she wanted a total break, a final goodbye because she said it was pointless for them to continue to be together. Neither of them would change.

Jake had had no problem facing down an enemy overseas, staring down a firefight. But Emily leaving was one thing he didn't want to think about.

Sunday night he went to her door to take her to her parents' house for dinner. When she opened the door, his heart thudded. She wore a red sweater, a red skirt and red pumps. Her hair was again in spiral curls, falling over her shoulders. He wanted to wrap his arms around her and kiss her all night.

"You look gorgeous," he said, getting his phone and taking her picture while she laughed.

"Come on, a selfie," he urged. She stepped beside him and he slid his arm around her waist and smiled as he took their picture.

"Okay, now I'll take you to your parents—unless we can go inside to kiss a little while first."

"Absolutely not," she answered and shook her head. "It's time to go. Everyone tries to get there on time. You look very nice in your sport coat and navy slacks. I like your black boots, too."

"Do I need a tie? I have one in the car."

"No, we're too casual for that. Actually, you don't even need your sport coat if you don't want to wear it."

"I'll keep it on. I'm trying to impress your family," he said, smiling at her. "I just would like to take you home with me later and peel you out of those clothes."

"Don't even think about it. At least not now." He took her arm to walk her to his car and the minute he touched her, he felt that spring of awareness at the contact. Their nights of loving hadn't changed that instant reaction they had to each other because he could tell from her quick breath that she felt it, too.

As soon as he was driving, she turned slightly to him. "Jake, since this next week will be my last at the Long L, I'd like to invite some people to come by and look at it if that's all right with you."

"Of course, it's all right. I've been thinking I might ask Ben Warner if he would like to see it. I don't think Camilla or Vivian will want to come. But Noah and Mike might. They don't have any bad memories of it, only curiosity. And I'll ask some neighboring ranchers when we get more livestock."

"I'll make sure everything's in order before I leave," she assured him.

Her departure was something he didn't want to think about. In fact, all he could think about now was how he was going to convince her to come back and go to bed with him. But he didn't think she would agree tonight. In fact, he'd have to mind his hands at her parents' house. Even though they hadn't talked about it, he felt certain she didn't want her brothers to know they were sleeping together, which was ridiculous.

When he drove up the winding drive in a gated area, there were cars lining the circular drive. Big shade trees and flower beds surrounded the three-story mansion.

The minute they stepped inside the wide hallway, he could hear voices and smell chili cooking. "Ahh, that dinner will be good."

"So will everything else," she said, smiling at him and linking her arm through his.

"Sure you want to do that?" he asked, looking at her arm. "Doug and Lucas will not approve."

"I'll tell you what, I can hold my own with my brothers."

He smiled. "I believe you there, but they know better, I'm sure, than to pound their baby sis. Well, let's go meet the happy family."

She looked at him intently and he wondered what she was thinking, but they entered the great room and were immediately the center of attention of a whole group of people of all ages and he forgot their conversation.

Emily took Jake around the room to introduce him to her parents, both sets of grandparents, and Andrea and Andrea's family. Sheila held her arms up, so Emily picked her up as she introduced Jake to her brother-in-law, James, and to Doug's wife, Lydia, who he'd missed meeting at the charity dinner.

Her brother stepped up. "Welcome to our family gathering," Doug said, offering his hand.

"Glad to have you," Lucas added, shaking Jake's hand next. "We want to come see the Long L sometime. Em's been telling us about the changes and all our lives we've heard about the Warner grandfathers that lived there."

"I can imagine. They were notorious in these parts. Come out this week while Emily is still there. We'll be glad to show you around. It looks very different."

"Are you settling there?" Lucas asked and Emily was curious about Jake's answer, watching him give a shake of his head.

"No. I'll stay there occasionally, but I love my Hill Country ranch and that's where I'll be most of the time unless I'm in Dallas."

"Excuse me," Emily said, "Mom is motioning for me." She left him with her brothers, having a feeling the talk would soon be about horses and rodeos.

The men gathered in a cluster, drinking beers and talking until dinner was announced. She joined Jake and sat beside him. Her family had questions about Jake's plans for the ranch. They moved on to other topics and when they laughed at a rodeo story Jake told, she felt a pang that he didn't want a family because he fit into hers easily. After dinner, all the adults played a word game and Jake seemed to enjoy himself, but even if he wasn't having a good time, she knew him well enough by now to know he could be very polite and pleasant when he needed to be.

Andrea and James were the first to leave because of the little kids.

Next, Emily took Jake's arm and they told everyone goodbye and Jake thanked her parents for dinner. As they walked to the car, he held her arm. "Too bad Thane couldn't see that. This is what he'd hoped for."

"Word will get around, you'll see. And you did quite well for a guy who doesn't spend time with family."

"Right now, the only person I want to spend time with is you," he told her. "Come to my condo and let me show you the view tonight. It's special."

She was silent a moment, knowing she was supposed to go to her place and that that would be the sensible thing to do. "Jake—"

He placed his hand on her nape, caressing her so lightly. The moment he touched her she wanted to be in his arms and kissing him.

"My place, okay?"

"Yes," she whispered, unable to resist because this was the beginning of the last week at the Long L for her. Next Sunday night Jake would be on his ranch and she would be in Dallas with the family, and she wasn't going to see any more of him. That hurt. From the first moment that they'd decided to do more than just work together, she had known that she would be hurt, but it had seemed far away in the future.

As they drove to his place, she fell silent, lost in thought. Jake had fit into her family tonight and he seemed to have had a good time, but she knew that he was making an effort because of his promise to Thane. His friend and half brother. She was certain Jake hadn't changed his feelings about families, marriage, kids. She forced herself to stop thinking about it when he pulled into his underground parking spot.

They rode up in silence and he unlocked and

opened his door, letting her go ahead. He followed her inside and reached out to take her arm.

She turned as his sport jacket fell on the floor behind him. He drew her into his arms and she went eagerly, wrapping her arms around him and kissing him as if tonight were their last time together.

There was a desperation in holding him. She held him against her heart, pressing her body against his until she leaned back a fraction to unbutton his shirt and pull it out of his trousers.

As she did, he peeled off her red sweater and tossed it on a chair. "I want you, Emily. You have no idea how much I've thought about you and how much I want you." He carried her to his bedroom, where a small lamp already shed a soft light in the room.

Jake stood her on her feet, looking into her eyes, and she couldn't get her breath. She thought he probably could hear her pounding heartbeat.

She stepped back, unfastening her skirt. As she wiggled her hips, her skirt fell around her ankles and she saw his chest expand from a deep breath.

While he shed his shirt, his hungry gaze was on her breasts in a skimpy lace bra and her lace panties that she still wore. She stepped out of her heels, watching him, wanting him more with every second. Next, she unfastened and tossed away her bra and removed the panties.

Watching her with a smoldering intensity, he finished undressing, turning to run his hands so lightly over her body.

"You're beautiful and I want to touch and kiss you slowly, so slowly," he whispered trailing light kisses from her throat to her breast. Then his mouth finally covered hers and his arm went around her waist to pull her against him, bare body against bare body. She gasped with pleasure and longing.

When he kissed her, she felt as if he would devour her. His hungry kiss made her heart race as his tongue went deep, thrusting over hers, possessive and demanding.

While he kissed her, he carried her to his room, yanking away the duvet and placing her on the bed. Kneeling on the mattress beside her, he showered kisses on her, circling each nipple with his tongue while his hands caressed her body with feathery touches. He ran his tongue lower, teasing, stirring her to want him desperately. Her fingers tangled in his thick hair while she arched her hips beneath him, giving him more access to her.

He shifted lower, the tip of his tongue running down between her legs. At the same time that his tongue stroked her, he caressed her slowly with his hands on her legs and belly.

With a cry, she sat up to push him down on the bed, moving over him to kiss him the way he had her. She ran her tongue over him, taking her time,

knowing she was exciting him and trying to pleasure him as he had her.

"Jake, I want you," she whispered. "Get a condom."

"Wait, darlin'. Just wait and let me love you."

"I've waited a lifetime for you," she whispered.
"I can't wait any longer."

He sat on the edge of the bed and picked her
up to set her astride him. With his hand stroking
her nape so lightly, he kissed her. As he did, his
other hand went between her legs to toy with her,
rub her and then slide his finger into her softness,
making her cry out and move on him.

"I want you," she whispered urgently, sliding off
him and standing to look at him. She stepped close
so he could take her breast in his mouth and run
his tongue over her nipple. While he teased her,
she trailed her hands across his muscled shoulders.

He picked her up to place her in bed and he
turned to get a condom, moving between her legs
to put on the condom as she watched him.

"I can't wait now," he said. "Next time tonight,
we'll take lots of time." He lowered himself, enter-
ing her slowly, and she felt a wave of sexual longing
sweep over her. She arched to meet him, running
her hands on his shoulders, then down his smooth
back as she thrust with him while he filled her.

She wrapped her long legs around him, her
hands squeezing his bare butt, trying to pull him

deeper, closer. Holding him, she cried out in passion and need.

He thrust hard and fast, making her move with him. They pumped and suddenly release burst over her with her climax so intense that she cried out in ecstasy. Holding him tightly and moving her hips fast with him, she tried to give him the same pleasure.

He pumped harder, faster and suddenly groaned, thrusting deeply and shuddering with his climax.

They slowed until he finally stretched beside her, one of his legs between hers as she ran her fingers in his hair. Her other hand stroked his smooth back that was damp with perspiration. "Jake, this is paradise."

He kissed her throat instead of replying, his left hand stroking her so lightly.

"You're fantastic," he whispered finally. "You'll never know how much I wanted you," he added. "Next time will be slow. I'll kiss you and caress you until you want me as desperately as I just wanted you."

She wrapped her arm around his narrow waist, to hold him close while she lightly kissed his ear and his neck. When he couldn't see her lips, she mouthed, "I love you," but that was all. She didn't whisper them.

She would never tell him she loved him. They had no future, only a short past. When they parted,

Jake would walk away with her heart and he would never even know it. She didn't want him to know. She had to let him go and tell him goodbye. For now, though, he was here in her arms and she could kiss him as much as she wanted.

Friday night, after working hard all week to complete her assignment at the Long L, she was packed and ready to go in the morning. Jake would fly her back to Dallas.

When Saturday morning came, as they left the ranch and walked out the door, he had his pickup waiting at the front. She asked him to wait while she walked into the fenced front yard and took a picture of the house.

She took two more and had three pictures of Jake standing with his pickup in front of the house. He had on a black Stetson, a black long-sleeve shirt beneath his denim jacket and tight jeans and he looked every inch the Texas rancher. She loved him with all her heart and she hurt badly. She knew she should cut the ties today, but she had agreed to stay Saturday night in Dallas with him.

They'd planned to have dinner out, but after they left the ranch, flew to Dallas and went to his condo, he took her into his arms to kiss her and they didn't leave his condo from that moment on.

Sunday morning she lay beside him with his arm around her. It was finally goodbye today. She had been awake a lot of the night, lying quietly beside him, sometimes caressing him until he would wake and they would make love again.

She ran her fingers across his muscled chest. "Jake, are you awake enough to talk?"

"I am now," he drawled and rolled on his side, propping his head on his hand to look at her and toy with locks of her long hair. "Actually, I was awake and I've been thinking about us. I know what you'll answer but I still want to ask, anyway. Will you move in with me, maybe go home with me to my other ranch part of the time?"

Her heart thudded. She could move in with him and hope he'd change his mind and want to make it permanent. As she thought about it, he remained quiet.

She hurt, but she knew the answer. "I can't do that, Jake. I guess that's old-fashioned, but so is my whole family. Old-fashioned and happy. Very happy. That's what I want and maybe someday, some guy will come into my life and share that, but if that doesn't happen, I can't change what I want and who I am."

"Your answer doesn't surprise me, but if I hadn't asked, I'd always wonder."

"As long as we're on the subject of families, relationships, love and the future, I'll admit I've been thinking about us. Really thinking about you."

"How so?" he asked, sounding amused as he turned to look at her.

"Jake, I'd never expect you to change. And know that I won't change. Intimacy to me is a precious thing between two people and vows are meant to be kept. If I have a long-running relationship, I have to have commitment. But there's no denying that there's something special between us, something unique that generates these crazy sparks that fly between us whenever we're together."

"Darlin', is there ever. I don't want to let you go."

"It's because of that fiery chemistry that I've made an exception these last few nights. Though I want commitment, I also wanted to let go and make love, kiss and be kissed, do things with you, because you're handsome, sexy, exciting—"

"If this is a goodbye, that isn't the way to do it," he said, his brown eyes intense, as he looked at her. His smile had vanished.

"It is goodbye and why I wanted this final time with you. I wanted to do those things with you that took me out of my world. I may never find the fire and excitement with anyone else that I've found with you but I'll wait, Jake. I've told you that I want a ring, a family, kids and dogs. I want it all. I can't have that with you, so I won't live with you on the ranch or in Dallas. We end today. You'll go on with life and you won't miss me because I've never been a real part of your life."

"I'm going to miss you terribly," he whispered and kissed away her answer.

An hour later, he lay with his arm around her, holding her close against him. She turned on her side to look at him, touching him lightly, her fingers playing in his curly chest hair.

"Jake, you've told me from the time we first met that you have a dim view of marriage because your own family has done so poorly. And your brothers and sister have warned you not to have kids because fighting for their custody will tear you up."

"That's right," he said, sounding amused. "Are you going to give me a pitch about how good it is in your family and I should rethink my stand on marriage?"

She didn't answer for a minute. "No, it's not my family I'm going to remind you about. It's your family."

"How so? What about my family?"

"You don't have Dwight Ralston's blood in your veins. He wasn't your dad. Your dad has been married only once and he still is married to the same woman, even if he did have an affair and had you out of wedlock. Your dad married for life and he was a good father. Your half brother Thane was happily married and loved his wife deeply. Have you stopped to think about that?"

"No, I didn't, because I wasn't raised in their family with their values."

"Whose idea was it that your two families live only two houses apart?"

"I don't know. I just figured that was coincidence," he answered. Hadn't it been?

And what did it mean that he had none of Dwight Ralston's blood in his veins? Not one drop. Since finding out the truth, he hadn't had much time to think about the implications.

Nor did he now.

The only thing that processed in his brain was the ominous warnings about marriage that his siblings had given him all his life.

"I'm not meant for marriage, Emily. My family isn't close. They don't enjoy each other's company and the kids haven't had the home life they should have had. That's the environment I've grown up in and I think that's the bigger influence than blood ties. So, nice try, but marriage and family—not for me."

She nodded, as if she accepted his response, but he could see the light dim in her eye. Then she quietly slipped out of bed. "I'm going to get dressed, Jake. It's time for me to go."

He had told women goodbye too many times. In the past, it had never bothered him, but now... Was he losing the best person he would know? And the best person to share his life with? When he asked himself that question, he knew marriage wasn't for him. He had known that since his mother's third marriage and all the upheaval her divorces caused.

He got up to shower and dress in the other bathroom so he could tell Emily goodbye when she was ready to leave. But as the water beat down on him, all he could think about was how much he was going to miss her. For the rest of his life, would he look back with regret for letting her go?

Ten

Jake waited in his living room until she came out of the bedroom. She wore tight jeans, a pink sweater that had an open V-neck and revealed her curves, and black boots that gave her more height, making her long legs look even longer. He wanted to cross the room, toss the bag in her hand into a corner and kiss her until she would let him carry her back to bed.

Instead, he took the bag from her. "The rest of your things are in the limo. I'll walk down with you, but I'm not riding to your house with you. We'll say goodbye at the limo. My driver will chauffeur you and carry your things in."

She nodded without saying anything. Her brown

eyes were wide and she was quiet. He placed his hands on either side of her face to look at her. Her hair was soft on his fingers and he hurt.

"I don't want you to go, Emily. If you ever change your mind and want to go out or come back and move in for a while, call me."

She smiled. "And get a new lady friend on the phone? I don't think you really want that."

He couldn't return her smile. He didn't want her to go. This was a first in his life and the pain in his heart was unfamiliar. "Emily, I want you. I can't marry and settle down and do Sunday night dinners, but have you thought that you might be happy with a man who loves you and comes home to you and wants to be with you?"

"Jake," she whispered and for a moment he thought maybe she was going to change her mind and accept his invitation to move in and stay longer. As he gazed into her eyes, she shook her head. "I just can't."

Nodding, he walked down to the limo with her and opened the door for her. Jake faced her, touching locks of her hair and letting his hand rest on her shoulder. "I'll look up your art gallery when you open one in Dallas. Better yet, send me an invitation and I'll come," he said and she nodded.

"Sure, Jake. I'll probably see you when the decorator works at the ranch, though I may be able to turn it all over to her with the plans I've drawn. If I don't see you again, I hope your ranches work out the way you want. Good luck with whatever you do. The old ranch house was interesting and I feel so fortunate for all that Thane has done. You take care of yourself," she said, stepping close and brushing a kiss on his cheek. "I'll miss you," she said. "Just remember your heritage."

"Sure. And if you want me, call me."

She just nodded. "Thanks for everything. I think you did a great job keeping the promises you made to Thane."

"I've tried and I'll keep trying and I appreciate your brothers' cooperation. Of course, you gave them an incentive."

When she made a move to enter the limo, he stopped her with a hand to her waist. She turned back to him and he felt as if his heart were cracking in two. "Emily, I…I'm going to miss you."

She shook her head. "No, you won't, Jake. You'll find a beautiful model or starlet and go on your way. Have a happy life, Jake. You've been very special," she added. Then she turned and climbed into the limo, stepping out of his life for good.

The limo pulled away from the curb and she glanced out the back and saw Jake standing there watching them drive away.

Hurting, she couldn't stop the tears that streamed down her cheeks and blurred her vision. She tried to control her crying until she got home, but she had to get a tissue and dab at her eyes. She loved Jake and thought he was wonderful. She hurt terribly and her gut said the pain was going to take a long time to get over. She had a feeling she would love him the rest of her life.

When they arrived at her home, the driver carried her things inside and left, and silence filled the empty house. Missing Jake, knowing it was going to be difficult without him, she stopped trying to stave off the tears and gave herself over to them. She cried like she'd never cried before, and she didn't stop.

She didn't want to join the family tonight; she suspected her brothers would guess right away what was bothering her and she didn't think she could hide it from them. She called her mother and said she was worn-out and was staying home tonight.

It was about nine o'clock when she got a text from Lucas. Sorry you're not feeling well. Can I come by? Mom sent dinner.

She wanted to text back saying no thanks, but she didn't. Instead, she sent him a text telling him to come by, that dinner sounded good, though in actual fact, she hadn't eaten and couldn't bear the thought of food. But she figured the bigger the fuss she made about being unable to join the family, the more Lucas would want to know what had really happened and then he would blame Jake. She didn't need her brother's interference in her life. So she combed her hair, wiped her eyes with a cold cloth and put on makeup, hoping it would conceal her red puffy eyes.

She heard his car and went to the door as Lucas rang the bell. She opened the inside door and then the storm door and held it.

"Come in and thank you for bringing dinner."

He came in and looked intently at her. "I'll put this in the kitchen. Sorry you're under the weather."

"I'm okay, just tired. The job is finished and we worked fast. Now I have a lot to catch up on tomorrow."

He set the dish in the kitchen and came back to face her. "Are you okay?"

"I'm very okay."

"I'm surprised he didn't ask you to move in with him."

"It's none of your business, but he did and I said no."

Lucas studied her. "That's good. Women are trophies to him."

"Lucas, don't. I—"

He put up his hands, palms out. "Okay. I'm going, I'm going." He stopped at the door and turned to her. "Want me to punch him out?"

"No, Lucas—" She realized he was teasing when he started laughing and she shook her head and forced a laugh. "By now, I should know when you're being ornery."

"At least you laughed. Seriously, I hope you're okay. Not many women walk away from Jake Ralston with their heart intact."

"Stop worrying. I'm fine."

"Sure," he said and left.

She closed the door behind him. "I love him," she whispered, wondering when it would stop hurting so badly. She missed him. How would she sleep tonight? She wanted his arms around her. She wanted him holding her close and kissing her. "I hope you miss me, Jake Ralston," she whispered. "Even half as much as I miss you."

She went to the studio she had set up in one of the spare rooms of her house, hoping that maybe drawing might assuage the pain. But all she managed to draw was his picture, even getting out her phone and selecting one of the photos of him that she could copy. The drawing pencil scratched across the pad furiously, until suddenly she stopped it. She missed Jake with all her being. She wanted his loving, his laughter. She could call him and move in with him and take life on his terms and maybe he would never want her to leave him.

The thoughts came out of nowhere but once she processed them, she knew she couldn't do any of that.

"Jake," she whispered and put her head in her hands to cry.

Through the sobs, a voice echoed in her head. How long would it take before she stopped loving him?

October in Dallas, and the weather was still balmy. Jake had been on his JR Ranch for two weeks, working hard outside, trying to forget Emily. Now he was back in Dallas temporarily. The Long L Ranch was as finished as he was going to get it unless he decided to live there part of the time. But he didn't like staying on that ranch because it held too many memories of Emily. It was the same at his condo in Dallas and even in his office. He tried to work, but too much of the time, he would realize he was staring into space, remembering when she was with him.

He couldn't get her out of his thoughts and that was a first. He had never had that reaction to any woman who had been in his life.

Causing him more worries today, at lunch he had run into Lucas Kincaid at a downtown restaurant. As Jake had approached the door, Lucas had come out and turned in the opposite direction.

"Hey, Lucas," Jake had called out, catching up with the man before he started to cross the street. "How's Emily?"

"She's great," Lucas had said, smiling and sounding friendlier than usual. "She's into her art and taking some time off just to have fun. She said she worked hard at the Long L and she's turning some of the store work over to one of the women who works for her. She's great, Jake. I think soon she'll have a location for her art gallery. She's very happy about her art. How's the Long L?"

"The ranch is fine. I'm staying more at my Hill Country ranch, but I had work here in town today."

"It's good to see you. I'll tell Em you asked about her. See you," Lucas had said and gone on his way.

The encounter had left Jake feeling more unhappy. If Emily missed him and was unhappy, Lucas would have been ready for a fight, not all smiles and cheer. Was there another guy already in her life? That thought turned him ice cold.

He didn't know what was happening in his life. From the first moment he'd met Emily, she had turned his world topsy-turvy and maybe captured his heart.

That was what worried him. He had gone with women, gorgeous, fun women he liked, and when they parted, he had said goodbye and never looked back. He had never hurt over ending an affair. Until now.

Now he couldn't work. He couldn't concentrate. He didn't want to go to the ranch, to his condo, to his office.

He missed Emily. He missed her to a degree that amazed him.

He'd worked out hours each day. That hadn't helped at all. Nothing helped and hearing Lucas today made him miss her even more. Had he made a mistake in telling her goodbye?

That night, again, he couldn't sleep. He sat in his big bedroom in his Dallas mansion, racked by images of Emily. Was he really in love for the first time in his life? The kind of love she talked about?

Jake stared into the darkness and pondered his discoveries. He had spent a lifetime thinking he came from bad blood, that he couldn't possibly stay married to one woman and that he wouldn't be happy in a marriage because his mother, his half brothers and the man he thought was his father hadn't been. But that man was a stepfather and those were half brothers just as Thane was a half brother, and Thane had had a great marriage. And his blood father had stayed in one marriage all his life. If only Thane were here and Jake could discuss it with his half brother and friend. What would Thane say?

Was Jake cheating himself of magical nights with a woman he loved because of mistakes others had made? He could imagine Thane's remarks on that one.

He remembered Ben Warner sitting on a little stool with a canvas seat that he took fishing and

showing him how to bait a hook and get it into the
water and then he remembered Ben being right
there with him, so enthused over the small bass
he'd caught in the pond.

In those moments, his dad had been there for
him. He'd had a father and a damn good one. At
the time, he had thought Ben was the closest thing
he had to a good dad, when actually Ben Warner
was his dad. His very good, reliable dad.

"Ahh, Thane, you and your father are my family. Half my family."

And right then he realized the lessons he'd
learned from the Warners.

And he knew he needed to talk to Emily.

Emily was up early, had made her three-mile
morning run and was in her art studio working on
her portrait of Jake. She had it sketched out and
was doing it in charcoal. At first, she'd thought
maybe the sketch would be cathartic, but not now.
She missed him and that hadn't eased at all.

She received a text and her heart missed a beat
when she saw it was from Jake.

Will you go to dinner with me tonight? I need to
ask you about something.

She stared at his message and wondered if his
question was personal or about the Long L Ranch.

It didn't matter. She wanted to see him. She wrote back instantly.

What time?

Pick you up at 7:00 p.m. Plan for hours and hours with me. Okay?

She smiled and her heartbeat sped up.

Okay. Make it worth my while.

Oh, what a challenge. I'll work on that one today.

She had to laugh at his answer. She knew it was one night, one dinner, but she was excited, happy she was going to see him. Who knew where it would lead.

"Maybe I'm not as easy to forget as you thought I was," she said aloud and then gave herself a lecture to not get her hopes up. For all she knew, he could want to see her about the ranch.

All day she couldn't calm her racing heart. Eagerness built as she went to the salon and had her hair done, and it tingled through her veins as she dressed in the new dress she'd bought. She couldn't wait for him to appear.

She heard a car and saw a long white limo out-front. Jake, looking very much a rancher, emerged. He wore a black Stetson, black boots, a black jacket and slacks and a white dress shirt with French cuffs, and her heart thudded because he looked incredibly handsome. She wanted to run and throw herself into his arms. He carried a bouquet of mixed red roses, white daisies and purple, yellow and pink lilies.

Smiling, Emily opened the door and waited.

Jake saw the door open and when Emily stepped out, his heartbeat suddenly raced. Any qualms or questions or second thoughts he'd been having on the drive to her house vanished forever. He wanted her in his life and he couldn't wait to tell her. He hoped with all his heart that he hadn't waited too long to make this decision.

He walked up to her and smiled, wrapping his arm around her tiny waist. "Darlin', let's go inside," he said, taking her with him and closing the door behind them. He turned her to face him.

"You cannot imagine how I've missed you. I want to talk to you."

"Oh, Jake, I—"

He placed his finger on her lips. "Shh. Listen to me. These are for you." He held up the flowers.

"They're beautiful."

He placed them on a nearby table, wanting her hands free for him to hold. "I've missed you, Emily. And I've thought about what you said about my family. My blood family. I thought about what Thane would have said to me if he were here so we could discuss my heritage. I think I know exactly what he'd say."

Her heart drummed as she looked into his brown eyes while he held her hands.

"He'd say go for it. That I deserve to be happy. Now, I know you want all the old-fashioned stuff, the wedding ring, the proposal. I have already gone to your dad and asked his permission to ask for your hand in marriage and he said yes."

Emily could only stare in shock. "You talked to my dad before you asked me?"

"Yes. I'm trying to be as old-fashioned as possible." As he talked, Jake went down on one knee and took her hand. "I, Jake Ralston, am asking you, Emily Kincaid, will you marry me?" He reached into his pocket, took out a box and held it out to her.

For a millisecond she said nothing, just stared at him, and his breath stalled in his throat. Would she say no?

"Yes, Jake, yes, I'll marry you," she said finally, a smile breaking out on her face. "And for heaven's sake, get up!" She laughed with joy and he was finally able to exhale.

Standing, he opened the box to show her the symbol of his love. The huge diamond surrounded by smaller diamonds on a gold band shimmered in the light. He took the ring out of the box and tossed the box as he took her hand and slipped the diamond on her finger.

Tears of joy filled her eyes before she threw her arms around his neck. "That is the most beautiful ring ever. I love you, Jake. Oh, how I love you. I've loved you since the first night with you."

He stepped back to look into her eyes. "You've been in love since then?"

"Oh, yes."

"Why didn't you tell me?"

"Because you didn't love me, and I didn't want you to worry or feel guilty. But it doesn't matter now. I love you and I'll tell you every day of the rest of my life."

He smiled and kissed her, a long seductive kiss, while she clung tightly to him and he picked her up and held her against him.

"I can't believe I'm saying this," he told her, "but I want a wedding soon."

She laughed again. "Sure thing, sweetie. A big traditional wedding with all our families, friends and relatives."

"That's right. I want Ben for my best man to stand in for Thane. With Ben standing near during our marriage, I'll know my real dad is right there with me wishing us a lifetime of happiness. And I want Mike and Noah as groomsmen and Lucas, Doug, Will and James. We're going to be family."

"Oh, Jake, it will take a lifetime to show you how much I love you. I can't believe you talked to my dad."

"Darlin', you like the old-fashioned life, so that's what it'll be. I'll do all the old-fashioned things I can—maybe not at bedtime, but otherwise. I love you, Emily. I love you with all my heart."

"Ah, Jake, my handsome fiancé, my lover, my future and my world. You're wonderful and you can't even begin to imagine how much I love you." Joyous, she held him tightly as she kissed him and set out to show him.

* * * * *

COMING NEXT MONTH FROM

♦ HARLEQUIN®
Desire

Available February 5, 2019

#2641 LONE STAR REUNION
Texas Cattleman's Club: Bachelor Auction
by Joss Wood
From feuding families, rancher Daniel Clayton and Alexis Slade have been star-crossed lovers for years. But now the stakes are higher—Alexis ended it even though she's pregnant! When they're stranded together in paradise, it may be their last chance to finally make things right...

#2642 SEDUCTION ON HIS TERMS
Billionaires and Babies • by Sarah M. Anderson
Aloof, rich, gorgeous—that's Dr. Robert Wyatt. The only person he connects with is bartender Jeannie Kaufman. But when Jeannie leaves her job to care for her infant niece, he'll offer her everything she wants just to bring her back into his life...except for his heart.

#2643 BEST FRIENDS, SECRET LOVERS
The Bachelor Pact • by Jessica Lemmon
Flynn Parker and Sabrina Douglas are best friends, coworkers and temporary roommates. He's becoming the hardened businessman he never wanted to be, but her plans to run interference did *not* include an accidental kiss that ignites the heat that has simmered between them for years...

#2644 THE SECRET TWIN
Alaskan Oil Barons • by Catherine Mann
When CEO Ward Benally catches back-from-the-dead Breanna Steele snooping, he'll do anything to protect the company—even convince her to play the role of his girlfriend. But when the sparks between them are real, will she end up in his bed...and in his heart?

#2645 REVENGE WITH BENEFITS
Sweet Tea and Scandal • by Cat Schield
Zoe Alston is ready to make good on her revenge pact, but wealthy Charleston businessman Ryan Dailey defies everything she once believed about him. As their chemistry heats up the sultry Southern nights, will her secrets destroy the most unexpected alliance of all?

#2646 A CONVENIENT SCANDAL
Plunder Cove • by Kimberley Troutte
When critic Jeff Harper's career implodes due to scandal, he does what he vowed never to do—return to Plunder Cove. There, he'll have his family's new hotel—*if* he marries for stability...and avoids the temptation of the gorgeous chef vying to be his hotel's next star.

HDCNM0119

*Flynn Parker and Sabrina Douglas are best friends,
coworkers and temporary roommates. He's becoming
the hardened businessman he never wanted to be,
but her plans to run interference did not include an
accidental kiss that ignites the heat that's simmered
between them for years...*

Read on for a sneak peek of
Best Friends, Secret Lovers *by Jessica Lemmon,
part of her Bachelor Pact series!*

They'd never talked about how they were always overlapping
each other with dating other people.

It was an odd thing to notice.

Why had Sabrina noticed?

Sabrina Douglas was his best girl friend. Girl, space,
friend. But Flynn felt a definite stir in his gut.

For the first time in his life, sex wasn't off the table for
him and Sabrina.

Which meant he needed his head examined.

After the tasting, Sabrina chattered about her favorite
cheeses and how she couldn't believe they didn't serve wine
at the tour.

"What kind of establishment doesn't offer you wine with
cheese?" she exclaimed as they strolled down the boardwalk.
Which gave him a great view of her ass—another part of her
he'd noticed before, but not like he was noticing now.

Not helping matters was the fact that he didn't have to wonder what kind of underwear she wore beneath that tight denim. He knew.

They'd been friends and comfortable around each other for long enough that no amount of trying to forget would erase the image of her wearing a black thong that perfectly split those cheeks into two biteable orbs.

"What do you think?" She spun and faced him, the wind kicking her hair forward, a few strands sticking to her lip gloss. He reached her in two steps. Before he thought it through, he swept those strands away, ran his fingers down her cheek and tipped her chin, his head a riot of bad ideas.

With a deep swallow, he called up ironclad Parker willpower and stopped touching his best friend. "I think you're right."

His voice was as rough as gravel.

"You're distracted. Are you thinking about work?"

"Yes," he lied through his teeth.

"You're going to have to let it go at some point. Give in to the urge." She drew out the word *urge*, perfectly pursing her lips and leaning forward with a playful twinkle in her eyes that would tempt any mortal man to sin.

And since Flynn was nothing less than mortal, he palmed the back of her head and pressed his mouth to hers.

Don't miss what happens next!
Best Friends, Secret Lovers *by Jessica Lemmon,*
part of her Bachelor Pact series!

Available February 2019 wherever
Harlequin® Desire books and ebooks are sold.

www.Harlequin.com

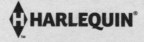